The Body Next Door

Steve Demaree

Steve Demaree

This book is dedicated to my wife of fifty-three years who has been a big help to me in my twenty-three years of writing books. She has helped me every step of the way. And it is dedicated to faithful readers and those who have been willing to help in proofreading and editing my books.

Steve Demaree

Books by Steve Demaree

Dekker Cozy Mysteries

52 Steps to Murder
Murder in the Winter
Murder in The Library
Murder at Breakfast
Murder at the High School Reunion
Murder at the Art & Craft Fair
Murder in Gatlinburg
Murder at the Book Fair
Murder on a Blind Date
A Body on the Porch
Two Bodies in the Backyard
A Body under the Christmas Tree
Murder on Halloween
A Valentine Murder
A Body on April Fool's Day
A Body in the Woods
A Puzzling Murder
A Body in Pigeon Forge
Murder Logically Speaking
The Unidentified Body
Wedding Bells and Murder
The Body Next Door

Sam Hendrix Mysteries

The Wrong Place
Mixed Up in Murder (will release around July 2023)

Meagan Morgan Mysteries

A Body in the Trunk

The Body Next Door

Murder at the Rialto (will release November 2023 or January 2024)

Other Mysteries

Picture Them Dead
Murder In A Gated Community
A Smoky Mountain Mystery
Murder In The Dark

Aylesford Place Series

Pink Flamingoed
Neighborhood Hi Jinx
Croquet, Anyone?
Scavenger Hunt

Non-Fiction

Lexington & Me
Reflecting Upon God's Word

Short Stories

Stories from the Heart

Steve Demaree

1

Hilldale had been murder-free for the last year. But just as the accident-free sign in a factory goes back to zero after growing to possibly three or four digits, Hilldale's nonexistent murder sign went from a round number to a straight or crooked one. That meant I had to go back to work. But first, I took an hour or so to reflect back over the last year to realize that a man (or a woman) of advancing age can still enjoy life if given the opportunity.

+++

Jennifer and I had a relatively good first year of marriage. We hugged and kissed a lot, and she never hit me over the head with her iron skillet. We discussed things and did whatever she wanted to do. Any man who tells you that he makes all the decisions is either kidding himself or has a bad marriage.

In general, Jennifer and I like the same things. For instance, neither of us likes murder, and neither of us likes solving them in person, which is my job, but we both love to read a good murder mystery. But when you narrow it down to specifics, we don't like the same things. In other words, we both like whodunits, but don't have the same favorites. We both like pizza but don't like the same toppings. She only likes pepperoni. I can add some sausage and extra cheese to mine, and some other things too. Just don't give me onions or mushrooms. She orders chicken at seafood restaurants, and I don't. We both like reading mysteries, watching TV series (mainly older ones), watching movies (again mainly older ones), and taking vacations. I'll share some specifics and start by sharing about our vacations because that's the first thing we did after saying our wedding vows.

We went on a three-week honeymoon, where our newlywed neighbors joined us in Gatlinburg for the last week of it. A few months later, we took another trip down to Gatlinburg, stayed a couple of weeks doing what we like there, which did not include climbing any mountains, and then came back home. As far as climbing mountains is concerned, a few years ago I trudged up to Clingmans Dome from the parking lot, taking a break on every rock on the way up. That excursion is definitely for someone younger and in better shape than I am. And I have lost over seventy pounds in the last few years. I doubt if I could have made it a quarter of the way up before I lost all of that weight. All the walking I have done with Jennifer has helped me lose that weight, although I lost most of it while we were dating, not after we married. I certainly didn't lose it dieting, although I have cut back considerably on what I eat when I'm not on vacation.

I say we vacation in Gatlinburg, because the place where we stay, Westgate, is one mile from Gatlinburg and three miles from Pigeon Forge. The Westgate property is over two hundred acres and the elevation at the top of the property is six hundred and fifty feet higher than at the entrance, and it is a mile of curvy road from the bottom to the top. Like any place to stay, there are pluses and minuses. I won't get into the minuses here, but the pluses are that the accommodations are better than in most places in Sevier County. They have two types of accommodations, which I will refer to as cabins and lodges. Both have several vacationers in a building, each with a private entrance. The cabins are three levels high, and you have to climb steps to get to each level. The lodges are four levels high and have an elevator. We have four weeks each year in a lodge. Two of our weeks include a living room, dining room, kitchen, bedroom with a jacuzzi, and of course, a bathroom. The other two weeks have a smaller living room and kitchen, a bedroom, and they too have a bathroom. Contrary to what you might have heard, some of Tennessee is civilized. The larger unit we stay in has a private balcony.

A nice thing about staying at Westgate is that they have a shuttle that will pick you up and take you anywhere on the property and the trolley stops at the entrance and will take you to Gatlinburg or Pigeon Forge, so you don't have to drive. We take the trolley to Gatlinburg because it is hard to find parking there without paying, but we drive to Pigeon Forge. Other amenities include multiple swimming pools, miniature golf, zip lining, restaurants, a water park, and a spa on the Westgate property. You can also pick up the phone and call a number if you need towels or ice, or if something breaks down, and someone will usually be at your door within thirty minutes. Now, there are minuses in staying there, but I won't get into them here.

A perfect trip to that area for me must include at least one breakfast at the Pancake Pantry in Gatlinburg, at least one round of miniature golf at Professor Hacker's Lost Treasure Golf, a trip to The Island in Pigeon Forge, where I must spend some time in the arcade and some time sitting on one of the rockers around the fountain. Also, time spent in the Old Mill District is a must. I need to go to the Old Mill Candy Kitchen to pick up some Bear Paws (chocolate, caramel, and pecans), and the Old Mill Creamery, where I will get a dish of banana pudding ice cream and one other flavor, or a sundae that includes hot fudge and caramel toppings, whipped cream, a cherry, and nuts. The Island and The Old Mill District are great places to meet people too. And they come there from many different states.

On our latest trip, we ate breakfast at Applewood Farmhouse, one of the top places for breakfast, where we had the sweetest server ever, Amanda Gomez. I thought she was in her early thirties, but she said she is forty-one. When I told her how sweet I thought she was, she started to cry. She told us to hurry back and ask for her. We will do that on our next trip down.

It had been a while since we took in a show at The Comedy Barn. Normally, I just smile when someone says something funny. But the ventriloquist and the man who has three men come up on stage and sit on three chairs had me laughing out loud. The ventriloquist was without a doubt the funniest ventriloquist I have ever seen. I've seen some talented ventriloquists (on America's Got Talent), but none are funnier than the guy at The Comedy Barn.

So, what do we like to do that doesn't include running a marathon or going on vacation? Well, we both like to eat, both at home when we are lazy or when the weather is bad, and out at some nice restaurants. We like to read mysteries, watch certain TV series, and watch movies, all of which can be done from our recliners or our couch. Yep, I'll admit it. I'm getting old. Oh, day trips to places in Kentucky are nice, even one to Cincinnati. My favorite place in Kentucky is Mammoth Cave. I love taking those cave tours. But the last time I took the four-and-a-half-hour tour, I told God that if He got me out of there alive I wouldn't do it again. He kept His part of the bargain, and so far, I've kept mine. I'm not even sure they still have that one. And to think, at one time they had an eight-hour tour. I wonder if they still have the lantern tour, where you crawl part of the way. I almost had to crawl part of the way on the one I took.

But we didn't sit around all the time as newlyweds. We did morning walks up the road that no one uses other than us and our next-door neighbors because there are no houses on the road after ours. And on those days when I'm feeling particularly chipper, we walk up the hill to the next house, although the next house backs up to the road rather than having its front facing the road.

On those days when we thought we should have some rain, the girls packed picnic baskets and we headed off somewhere. They packed enough food for eight, just in case we ran into some squirrels or birds. Lou's job was to pray that we didn't run into any squirrels or birds so there was more food for the menfolk. One time Jennifer caught on to our trick and invited our dog Blue along. Lou and I had to fight to get a couple of bites. We only managed that because there are a couple of things Blue doesn't eat. Sometimes he takes a duck bag home to Quiggley, the duck that adopted us. I try to go through it first to see if there is anything in there that I might want.

2

Jennifer and I are each compiling lists of our favorite TV shows, popular songs, movies, and mystery novels. I knew that our lists wouldn't match, but they wouldn't be as different as most married couples' lists would be.

I am not someone who can sit down and read an entire book in a day, which means there was no way I could reread the fifteen hundred or so books I've read since I became a serious reader again so that I could compile my list. So, I was thankful that I rated each book when I read it. I knew that my opinion of some books might have changed over the last twenty years, but I would go with my original rating of each book and choose the 100-150 books I rated the highest, but choose no more than three books or so by any author.

But I knew that I could choose 200-300 songs in a day or two and listen to all of them two or three times in a week or two to pick my favorites, possibly in order, so that would be easier than picking my favorite book. I would list my books chronologically in the order they were written, but I would choose my favorite songs in the order I liked them. That meant TV shows and movies would take the most time. I could come up with my favorite TV shows in each category in a couple of months, while it would probably take me close to a year to come up with my all-time favorite movies in order because I would have to rewatch them.

So, many months ago, we began by watching TV series. We watched over one hundred and fifty of them, but that is misleading. There were a few series that we could tell in a few minutes or after one episode that that particular series was not going to be anything we would like. Others we watched a season or more.

One thing that Jennifer and I agree on is that our favorite two types of TV shows that are on DVD are Crime shows and Comedies. We don't mention the "S" word (streaming) because I don't know how to do it, and the last time Jennifer mentioned it in Lou's presence he started singing *Down By The Old Mill Stream*. Because he knew we didn't like him singing it, he did a rendition that would have gotten him buzzed off *America's Got Talent* in less than five seconds. But I'm not up on streaming, Instagram, Tik Tok, and a lot of other things they didn't have when I first got a computer, which wasn't a *Commodore 64.*

But I'm pretty sure Jennifer's three favorite shows are *Rizzoli & Isles. NCIS,* and *Friends.* I think she could watch all three of them all day and night. Maybe for an entire week.

We saved listening to a week or two of songs until a time when the weather forecast was one when it was better to stay indoors for the next several days. When that time came, I took the first floor and Jennifer took the second one. Even though neither of us was a teenager during the 1960s (I was born after the decade started, and Jennifer wasn't born yet), both of us prefer music from that decade. But not always the same music. While we both love Neil Diamond, she leans more toward Gary Puckett and Bobby Goldsboro, whereas I like the Mamas and the Papas, Johnny Mathis, The Lovin' Spoonful, and Herman's Hermits. As I got older, I began to appreciate the Beatles more, as long as my friend from childhood and next-door neighbor Lou wasn't singing their songs. We both looked through a book that listed all of the popular songs from 1955-1985 and we each made a list of all the songs that could make our Top 100. I counted my list when I finished. It had 247 songs on it, including a couple that fell outside of that thirty-one-year range. I thought I could listen to all of them in a week. I might have been able to do that if I listened day and night, but I wanted to spend some time with Jennifer, so I only listened during the day and one night. Every three or four songs, I would put them in order. When I finished, I looked at the Top 125. I took a break of about six weeks and listened to them again in order, to come up with my final list. Jennifer did the same and we compared lists. There were some similarities, but a lot of differences.

It took us a few days after we finished listening to them for the first time to stop singing them, and only a couple of times did we make a mistake and sing in Lou's presence. But other than that, it was sort of fun. Sometimes one of us would sing a line from one of our favorites and the other one would sing the next line, or he or she would counteract by singing something that was an answer to that line from another song. A few times, after we had finished listening for the day, or during our several-week break, Jennifer and I would listen to a song and dance to it. We danced both slow and fast dances. Those fast ones were great exercise, especially for someone my age. Huffing and puffing at the end is not desired.

Jennifer and I try to vary what we do. So, after filling our heads with a lot of noise, it was time to quiet down and read. There is nothing like picking up a great book, one where you want to keep turning the pages or swiping across the tablet. Sitting on a front porch swing, lying on a chaise lounge on the back deck, or in a hammock with a gentle breeze blowing and no one around is perfect. Or lying in your recliner, on the couch, or in bed, if you can do that and read more than a couple of pages before falling asleep, is pure joy. I never fall asleep while reading. Sometimes Jennifer does.

While Jennifer and I both prefer mystery novels to any other kind of book, I've been reading them longer than she has. David Baldacci, Michael Connelly, and Lee Child have written so many books that she seems to rotate between those three. Now and then she reads someone else I recommend that I think she might like. I read all of those authors too, but I'm further along in each of their books than she is. I've read all of Child's books and most of the other two. I'm about halfway through Louise Penny's books. I like the ones set in Three Pines village in Canada better than the ones where her detective goes somewhere else. I also enjoy Hank Phillippi Ryan and have read almost all of hers. We always take books with us when we go to Gatlinburg and read a lot at home too. On vacation, we read in late afternoons, or after we return from dinner out. And when we are down there for two weeks, we have some days when we stay in and read. Usually rainy ones. I get a lot of books for Christmas. I really enjoyed two that I got this past Christmas, *The Judge's List* by John Grisham, and *Not A Happy Family* by Shari Lapena. I'm two-thirds of the way through one of Ryan's books that looks like it will be one of my favorites.

I try a few authors that are new to me each year. Some I add to my favorites list, and some I don't like.

But we devoted most of our time trying to find out our all-time favorite movies. When we got around to watching movies, we were all in. We have a movie collection of somewhere a little over one thousand. Over the year, we watched somewhere around four hundred movies. I think the most we watched in one day was five. Of course, some days we didn't watch any, like when we went on vacation or somewhere on a day trip.

In the first week, we watched twenty-four movies. Almost all of them were movies I had seen before. Some of them I had seen enough that I could quote dialogue. Unlike books, there are some movies I can watch every year or two.

As is the case with TV shows. Our favorites are Crime and Comedy, with some Action thrown in too. Over the year, we had days when we watched several movies of the same genre all day long. For instance, one day we watched three crime movies that were made before the movie rating system took effect in 1968; *Wait Until Dark, Dial M For Murder,* and *Witness for the Prosecution,* while another day we watched three that were made after that date; *The Bedroom Window, Suspect,* and *Double Jeopardy.* I would highly recommend all six.

On three other days we did the same with comedies, like *No Time For Sergeants, Some Like It Hot,* and *Pillow Talk* in one day, and *Seems Like Old Times, The Secret of My Success,* and *Weekend at Bernie's* on another day. On the third day, we watched *Tootsie, Mrs. Doubtfire,* and *Kind Hearts and Coronets.* And we also took a few days to see which James Bond we liked the best and whether we preferred James Bond movies or *Mission Impossible* movies.

I watched all of the movies through the closing credits. I loved watching the names of those who worked on the movie that people have never heard of, especially those with unusual names. Particularly those with long names. Greek, Italian, Polish, and Russian names were my favorites.

We snacked while we watched movies. Not a snack with each movie, but one snack a day, usually in the late afternoon. Most of the time it was popcorn with butter. I loved the smell. And some of the time I had a candy bar with it, either a Hershey Almond or a Maple Bun. But we ate ice cream, sometimes with syrup, whipped cream, a cherry, and nuts.

Before we started watching movies, I thought about what we would watch. I knew Jennifer and I wouldn't have the same favorites, although we would share many of the same ones. But I concentrated on my favorites. While mysteries and thrillers were my favorites followed by comedies, action movies were right up there with them. But would any musicals make my list? Unlike some men, I do like some musicals. But what would be my favorite? Would it be *The Sound of Music, Singing in the Rain, West Side Story, The Music Man,* or something else? And what about westerns? Would my favorite be one starring John Wayne, Clint Eastwood, or someone else? And would I like one or more well enough to put it in my Top 100 movies? I'm not a big science fiction or horror fan, but I do like the *Star Wars* movies and some of those black-and-white sci-fi movies of the 1950s, and some of those horror flicks of the 1930s. Would any of those make it? And I wasn't forgetting family movies and animated movies. How would *Sleeping Beauty* compare to *Beauty and the Beast?* And how did they compare to the Minions? And I was sure something with Hayley Mills would make my list, although most of her movies came out a few years before I was born. And while this isn't enough for a movie to make my list, what movie has the best opening scene? Is it *Raiders of the Lost Ark,* or one of the James Bond movies? And what actor and actress would appear most in movies that will make my list? I was going into this with an open mind. Four hundred or so movies later, I found out there were some movies I liked better than I used to, while there were others I didn't like quite as well. But my tastes still included movies of just about every type. And every decade.

+++

But I don't spend all of my days sitting around except when I'm on vacation. Shortly after Jennifer and I married, she started us on a new regimen.

I did not want to give up eating, so Jennifer strongly suggested that we begin each day with exercise. My Wii kept breaking more often than I wanted, which caused me to have to buy a new one. The money was no problem, but it was a pain to wait until a new one arrived or drive around until we could find a store that had one. There aren't a lot of stores in Hilldale that sell Wiis. There aren't a lot of people in the world who still use them. So, Jennifer suggested that we walk each day. Every day. Rain or shine. Unless there was lightning.

And so we walked. On the first rainy day, I reached for an umbrella. Jennifer said we didn't need one. I admit she did look good wet. Even soaked. On the second rainy day, I suggested taking a bar of soap. She laughed but made me put it back. So we walked through the meadow, through the woods, and up the road that no one uses but us. On sunny days, on cloudy days, through rain puddles, and even when we made tracks in the snow. We walked and if the conditions weren't to our liking, we laughed as we endured. Quiggley liked the rainy days. Mondays too. They didn't get her down. Sometimes we sang. Based on the weather. *Sunshine On My Shoulder, Singin' in the Rain, White Christmas, Jingle Bells.* It made our walks more fun. Even the time we fell down in the mud. When it snowed and we sang *Jingle Bells* I suggested to Jennifer that we get a horse and a sleigh. She suggested Clydesdales. I told her I wasn't a beer drinker. She said we didn't have anywhere to keep a horse. I told her we could keep it at the newlywed's house next door. She said she liked her newlywed cousin too much to do that to her. I still don't have my horse, so I'm not as exuberant now when I sing *Jingle Bells.*

When we get back each day, we shower, even if it was raining when we walked. Then it is time to spend time with God. We pray together and separately. I read daily devotionals from four Daily Guideposts yearbooks. My two favorite devotional authors are men who were nothing like I am. One is Van Varner, a man who never married, and lived in a New York City apartment with his dog. The other is Oscar Greene, a black man who lived in Boston. I also enjoy reading Bill Irwin, a blind man who hiked the Appalachian Trail with his dog. But my favorite devotional book is *Reflecting Upon God's Word*. And of course, I read the Bible. Jennifer reads at the same time as I do, and then we both reflect on what we read.

Not only do we need direction from God, but we need to start each day off with a smile on our faces. I try to get inspiration from my favorite philosopher. Snoopy. And we read a few pages from *The Complete Far Side* by Gary Larson. One day I flipped pages in that book for an hour. Then it was time for Jennifer to fix her breakfast buffet. I help her by staying out of the way. She says it's one of my best attributes. After we eat, it is time to begin our day, however, we choose to spend it. We don't want to get in a rut, so we don't spend it the same way every day.

3

Most of you know that I'm not always a traveler, a reader, a TV watcher, or a bum. Sometimes, I'm a homicide detective. I change from Cy Dekker, husband extraordinaire to Lt. Cy Dekker, solver of all murders. And I take along my next-door neighbor, my friend from childhood, and an albatross, Sgt. Lou Murdock, who is a greater help when he is not heard or seen. I have no phone booth to change from one character to another, so I have to do it by receiving a phone call from the Chief of the Police Department, who only calls me when someone is murdered.

"Good morning, Cy."

It wasn't until I heard those words that I knew I shouldn't have answered the phone. I knew the Chief wasn't calling me to tell me no one was dead or to invite me over for dinner. But I had picked up the phone, so I had to respond.

"This is George. Cy's impersonator. Cy is no longer at this number. He went away on an around-the-world cruise and there is no telling where he is now."

"I have a good idea where he is, and I will arrest any impersonators and take them away from their wives."

"Chief, you never call me for any good reason."

"Yes, I do. To get murderers off the street."

"Train some younger person to do that."

"No one is as good as you."

"I have to agree with you there. Just hire twice as many detectives to do the job. I'm getting old."

"I did hire twice as many. Jennifer and Thelma Lou will help you solve the murder in no time at all. Besides, the body is at the house next door to your house."

"Lou's dead? Why didn't you say so? I can solve the case in half the time if he isn't around to hinder me."

"Lou isn't dead, and you know it."

"Well, if he's a widower, he'll be grieving, so he won't want to come with me."

"He won't be grieving."

"I think he loved Thelma Lou."

"He probably still does. She's still alive as far as I know."

"You mean there's a body in his house and he doesn't know it. That sounds like him."

"Wrong house, Cy. I'm talking about your house in town."

Reality hit me.

"Don't tell me it was a sexy woman in a bikini found floating in the water."

"You mean you already knew about it before I called?"

"You mean it was Annabelle?"

"So, she called you before she called us?"

"Who called me before she called you?"

"Annabelle. The sexy young woman in the bikini."

"Dead women don't use the phone much. They don't even text, which is something I don't do either."

"According to Frank, who is already there, Annabelle is the sexy young woman in a bikini who called us and said she came home, changed into her bikini, and went out and found out someone was already occupying her new pool, only she was dead."

"So, Annabelle is all right?"

"According to Frank, she is more than all right. He even said he can handle it by himself. He's okay with trying a live body for a change. But I told him to stick with the dead ones and I would call you. As for Annabelle, she is as all right as someone can be after coming home to find a dead person in her pool. You need to get over there and find out what you can."

"And console her. And there's no need to bother Lou or Jennifer," I said.

"I thought Lou was married to Thelma Lou."

"He is, but I'm not worried about her."

"Don't bother Lou or Jennifer about what?"

I noticed the question wasn't coming from the phone. I looked up to find my wife had just returned from visiting the neighbors, a little too soon to suit me.

I took my hand and motioned that I was on the phone, which she already knew. She could see the receiver from my bulky house phone up next to my ear.

"I'm on it, Chief. Listen, Jennifer just got back from visiting with the neighbors who aren't dead. I've got to go."

I hung up my old-fashioned house phone and looked for a hole to crawl into. I couldn't find one. In case I forgot what she said, Jennifer repeated her question.

"Don't bother Lou and Jennifer about what?"
"Don't bother Lou and Jennifer about anything."

"Let's try this again, Cy. Don't bother Lou and Jennifer about what?"

"Oh, nothing. There's been a murder, and the Chief thinks I can handle this one on my own."

"How good-looking is she?"

"The victim? Frank said she's a looker."

"Just where is this victim?"

"The Chief said it is at the house next door to mine."

"I was just there. Lou and Thelma Lou look fine. Are you saying someone dropped off a body around back?"

"This isn't my house."

"It's good of you to realize that it's mine now that we're married."

"Actually, it still belongs to the Foundation, but I do have a house in town."

"And the body is at the house next to that one?"

"It is."

"Is it at the house I'm familiar with?"

"I thought you were familiar with both of the houses. You've seen both of them."

"But I'm more familiar with a resident in one of those houses than I am with the other."

"Well, it's the one you're more familiar with."

"Well, you don't seem all that broken up, so I assume the deceased is a male."

"You assume incorrectly. Remember what the Chief said. It was a gorgeous young woman in a bikini."

"I didn't hear that part of the conversation. I'm sorry, Cy. You seem to be taking this well."

"Well, I am married to you, not Annabelle."

"Cy, you know I was kidding about her. I really did like her."

"I'll be sure to tell her that when I see her. I'm sure she will be glad to hear it."

"You mean she isn't the gorgeous dead woman in the bikini?"

"No. She is the gorgeous woman in a bikini who is still alive. The one the Chief wants me to go talk to so I can find out what I can for the case I now have to solve."

"So, she's not dead. She just has a dead woman in her house. Cy, I don't mean Annabelle's one of my favorite people. But then it has been a while since I've seen her. It would be good to see her again since you're going. Maybe I can be the one to talk to her while you talk to Frank."

"I think I can handle her on my own."

"I'm sure you can. That's why I'm going along. I'd hate for you to end up in the hospital. Should we bother the neighbors or go by ourselves? After all, they might have something else to do."

"Since you want to go along, I think maybe we should invite them so Thelma Lou can keep you out of trouble."

+++

We went to collect the neighbors. Lou already had his shoes on, since God had already given him the clue of the day. He wasn't all that happy about it, but he wasn't blaming God. He knew it was the murderer's fault.

"Okay, Hot Shot. You seem to know why we are here. What's today's clue?"

"Water, water everywhere, and not a drop to drink."

"There's been a flood."

"There has been. And God caused it, and we're not going to arrest Him. He was one of the few good guys."

"But why did he save so many insects?"

"He didn't. He saved only two of each kind. It's just that they went forth and multiplied."

"And some of them have had it in for me."

+++

We got in the van and Lou turned the radio on. The Standells were singing *Dirty Water*. I hoped that didn't mean we have to go to Boston to solve the murder. I headed toward town. Things didn't get any better. Otis Redding was *(Sittin' on) The Dock on The Bay*. That one was followed by Simon and Garfunkel's *Bridge Over Troubled Water*. Lou started singing. "When you're weary, feeling small. When tears are in your eyes." Tears were forming in my eyes, but it was because Lou was singing so badly. I looked around for dogs storming my van, but we were still far enough away from civilization that I saw none. The sloth I saw couldn't keep up. I was glad we didn't have to cross any body of water on the way to find out what we could about the deceased. But I was afraid of where we might go next, so I turned the radio off. I should have left it on. An awful noise started coming from the other front seat. More singing. And song Lou could think of that had to do with water.

+++

We arrived at the house where I used to live. I didn't want Lightning to get jealous, so I parked out front on the street and let my yellow VW have the driveway to herself. I think she appreciated that. I suggested to Jennifer that she go inside and make sure the house I used to live in was the same as the last time we were there. I had long ago removed the posters of Jennifer Aniston, Jennifer Garner, Jennifer Lopez, and Jennifer Lawrence. She said I knew the house a lot better than she did, so maybe I should check out my former abode while she solved the case.

I walked toward the house next door, off to question Annabelle. Jennifer, always helpful, directed me toward Frank instead. I refrained from letting Jennifer know that Annabelle was much more my type than Frank was. I noticed Annabelle was wearing a bikini. Jennifer did too. She grew more determined in her steering. I hoped that Frank was not attired in the same way as Annabelle and the dead woman.

I whispered to Lou to see that Jennifer didn't cause any harm to Annabelle's body, and then I continued on the path Jennifer meant for me to take. I pushed the sliding glass door open and looked at a woman lying beside the pool. She was a brunette, wearing a black bikini, still wet from her time in the pool. I had no idea how long she had been there. It was hard to tell, but I guessed she was someone in her mid-thirties. She looked like she had seen better days. I was greeted by the medical examiner.

"So nice of you to come, Cy. It looks like the body has deteriorated quite a bit while we were waiting on you."

"I think most of that was while it was waiting on you. What do you say was the cause of death?"

"I'm going with the end of life."

"Did someone help her end her life?"

"My guess is yes. But I'll know more after we've spent some time together."

"Do you mean you and me or you and her?"

"Her. I don't want to spend any more time with you than necessary."

"I'm glad you want to spend more time with her than necessary. Do you have any idea how long she's been dead?"

"Let's just say it didn't just happen. It's been long enough that I can't be accurate as to the time of death. But I'll give you the best effort I can. Now, I'm ready to load her up and take her away. I'll be able to tell you if she drowned, and if not, if she was killed here or somewhere else, but it will be up to you to find out who did it. By the way, I was beginning to like you. It's been a while since you made me go to work."

"I know this is hard for you to understand, Frank, but I've never made you go to work. I've never murdered any of the corpses you've come to collect. But I know how much all of them mean to you, and you've missed adding to your collection, so welcome back to the fold."

"This may come as a surprise to you, but I don't collect them. I just cut them up and make a stab at how they died, then pass them off to the mortuary, so people who haven't said anything good about them in a long time can make up for lost time. And I haven't been without work to do. Just without having to see your face, and that has been a lot of fun."

"I've enjoyed that part too. And not having to go out and solve all these murders."

"Well, at least now you have Jennifer to solve them for you quicker."

"Speaking of Jennifer, I'd better get inside. She and Annabelle don't exactly exchange Christmas cards."

"Cy, it's not the time of year for that. But I bet Jennifer has already complimented her on her outfit today."

"If she hasn't, I'll be sure to do just that. As long as Jennifer is out of the way."

"Just don't frisk Annabelle. I might not like the next detective as well as I like you."

I laughed and walked inside.

Jennifer saw the smile on my face.

"What's so funny?"

"Oh, Frank is always cracking jokes."

'Want to share this one with me?"

"Some other time. Now, I have to question the person who found the body."

"I'll get her number for you, my love."

"That's okay. She's just in the other room. And it's easier to question her in person."

"I bet it is. Okay, I'll watch from the doorway. And remember, so many times, the one who finds the body is the murderer."

"I'll remember to give her your regards."

4

I walked into the next room and noticed how good Annabelle looked in turquoise. Well, almost in turquoise. I'd have to ask her where she bought her ensemble so I could get Jennifer one just like it.

"Mrs. Oxley. We meet again."

"Cy, you remember my last name. I'm impressed. You're looking good. Lost a lot of weight."

I wanted to tell her I was impressed with her too, but I wasn't sure where Jennifer was. So, I toned it down just a bit.

"So are you, Annabelle. Do you usually dress this way for the police?"

"Only if *you* are one of the police. But I didn't realize that you were bringing your wife with you."

"Which reminds me, where's Derek?"

"We just got back in town. He went to pick up our mail and some lunch since we don't have anything to eat at the house. Naturally, we stopped the mail while we were gone. He thought we might have gotten something important while we were away. He should be back in a few minutes. I don't know how he will take it about me finding a body in our new pool."

"Actually, he won't have to take it. Frank is taking it away as we speak."

She laughed, which encouraged me. I turned and saw Jennifer, who wasn't quite as encouraged, so I resumed my questioning.

"Does Derek know about this?"

"I tried to call him, but evidently he was on the phone with someone, in the post office, or ordering food."

"And why have you dressed so attractively?"

"We unloaded from our trip. I decided to take a dip in our new pool. That's when I discovered the body and called you guys."

"I like the pool. How long have you had it? And do most of them come with a dead body these days?"

"A little over a month, and we didn't pay extra for the body. To tell you the truth, I'm a little unnerved by all of this. And as you know, it takes a lot to get to me. Most of the bodies I come across are in books that Derek and I read. Or write."

I had forgotten that she and Derek write mystery novels.

"Did you recognize the victim?"

"I just saw her briefly. I might have screamed, then run and grabbed the railing to catch my breath. I'm not sure. As soon as I was okay, well, as okay as I was going to get, I called and reported it. About ten minutes later, the first guy showed up. I think he said his name was George somebody or other. He said you would probably be showing up soon. Then the Medical Examiner came. They had me look at her after they checked her out to see if I knew her. As far as I know, she wasn't anyone I've ever seen."

"Were you and Derek away on one of your house swaps?"

"We were."

"Where were you?"

"The other side of Wilmington, North Carolina, over near the ocean, close to the Outer Banks. We went down the northern route through West Virginia. We came back by way of the southern route through Asheville and Knoxville. We spent a couple of days in Asheville and a day in Pigeon Forge. So, we took our time coming home."

"When did you leave eastern North Carolina?"

"Late Saturday morning."

"And how long were you at the home swap?"

"Just a week this time. But we spent a few days here and there on the way down."

It was Wednesday morning. They had taken a long vacation.

"Did you enjoy yourselves?"

"We did until we got home. Well, until I found the body. Derek may still be enjoying himself."

"So, you have no idea how someone got into your house and in your pool and drowned?"

"Isn't that where you come in, Cy?"

"I'm afraid so."

"And you don't know if this could be the person you swapped homes with?"

"We swapped with another couple. We had a picture of them. I'm pretty sure this isn't the woman. The other couple was older than us, probably around fifty. I only got a glimpse of this woman, but I don't think she made it to fifty."

"I think I have to agree with you there."

I was trying to think of any other questions I might have when we were interrupted.

"I got the mail and some lunch, Annabelle. You won't believe the phone call I got while I was out. Oh, hi, Cy. What's going on? And who these cars belong to, the police?"

"Hi, Derek. Maybe a murder."

"I know. But how did you know about it? The body was found at the place where we stayed in North Carolina Why would that concern you?"

"Another one was found here. That concerns me. Well, it concerned the Chief enough to send me here."

"Here? You mean like at our house?"

"The same. In the pool. And you say you left another body when you checked out of the house you stayed in for a couple of weeks?"

"We didn't check out. And the body wasn't there when we left the other day."

"Well, one just left here, and I doubt if it was the same body."

"Well, the guy who lives at the place where we were in North Carolina said the police are there now, checking things out. I even had to talk to that detective and answer a few questions for him."

"Did he tell you where they found that body?"

"No. Where did you find this one?"

"In the pool. Weren't you listening?"

"You mean someone contaminated my pool before I could use it? Was it a man or a woman?"

"A woman."

"In a bikini, Derek," Annabelle interjected.

"Was she pretty?"

"Men!"

"Well, was she?"

"Yes, she was young and pretty."

I wanted to get back in charge of the investigation, so I made sure Derek and Annabelle didn't discuss the woman in the pool.

"Annabelle said it wasn't anyone you knew."

"I only know one young and pretty woman in a bikini."

"You can't make up for it now," Annabelle broke in again.

"Who said I was talking about you?"

"Cy, if your wife wasn't here, I would ask you to take me away."

"Let's get serious again. I'll get in touch with the detective down in North Carolina and see what I can find out about that case. We'll know soon if this was a murder or a simple drowning, and if it was murder, learn if the woman was murdered here or somewhere else. I'll let you know if I have more questions.

"Oh, one other thing. Did the couple who was doing the home exchange with you make it to your house?"

"They did. He told me they left here on Saturday, and they stopped off at a few places on the way home too. They too just got home, found a body, and called the police as soon as they did."

"And where did they put the key when they left?"

"Around back, under a stone near the pool."

"Check and see if it's there."

I waited for him to check. I could tell by the way he looked when he came back that the key was missing.

"So, it's not there."

Oh, it was there all right, but on top of the stone."

"That's odd. When you call him and tell him about the murder here, ask him if he left the key on top of the stone. By the way, how many people know where you leave the spare key and that you would be gone for a couple of weeks?"

"Only a few friends. But those same friends knew someone would be staying here, so they wouldn't be stopping by."

"Anything else you can think of?"

Only that it's too bad this wasn't a scene in one of our books."

Again, I had forgotten that Derek and Annabelle write mystery novels together, even though Annabelle had mentioned it before Derek got home. I wondered what was going through their minds.

"And I want the two of you to check the house to make sure nothing is missing. We're not sure if they got in the house or just in the pool. Of course, it could be the woman just wandered in for a swim and drowned. She might not have been murdered. We'll know more after the autopsy.

"One more thing." I was beginning to sound like Lt. Columbo. "Do you know anyone who might have something against either of you?"

"No one I can think of. Can you think of anything, Annabelle?"

"No, I try to be nice to everyone."

She smiled at me when she said it. I tried not to let it faze me.

"First, we'll see how she died. If she was murdered, we'll have to find out who she is, find people who know her and get a list of people you know. Welcome home. Now you'd better eat your lunch. And our people should be through with your pool later this afternoon."

"I'm not sure when I'll want to get back in there."

"You need to dive in. You paid a lot of money for it. And I doubt if someone is in there waiting for you. And call me if you find anything suspicious or think of anything that might be helpful. I'll contact you if it turns out to be murder."

5

I gathered the troops, and we walked out. There was nothing else we could do regarding the investigation at that time. We would have to wait until Frank completed his autopsy. I knew that he thought it was murder. So did I. But was the woman murdered at Derek and Annabelle's house, and if so, when? I knew them well enough that I didn't think either of them murdered her. But what about the couple who traded houses with them for a week? And if it wasn't them, then who gained access to the house, how did they do it, and when? I knew Frank wasn't concerned about that. That would be part of what Lou and I would have to come up with. Well, the girls might help too. Sometimes Jennifer comes up with a good idea. Thelma Lou just goes along with the crowd.

I debated as to whether or not to pay a visit to my old homestead, but there was one matter more pressing. I needed to consult with the only detective who lives on the street. My pint-size neighbor that I don't see much anymore. Joey wouldn't be afraid of being questioned by four people he knows, so we all headed across the street to his house. For a change, his mother answered the door. I had expected him to come storming out the front door and tackle me in the street. I found out why. Joey was in the backyard. I knew there had to be some reason why we hadn't been charged by a tornado, and that was why.

The back gate squeaked as I opened it. The sound alerted a small boy high up in a tree, who descended from that tree much quicker than I could have at any age.

"Mr. Cy, did you come to invite me to a sleepover on your front porch in the woods? That way I can let you know if any bears come out of the woods."

"Not after the poor job you did at being a detective today."

"Something happened today?"

"The police stormed the house across the street and took a body away from Derek and Annabelle's swimming pool, and you didn't even call me to let me know they are here. I had to find this out from the Chief. What kind of detective are you?"

"You're kidding me, aren't you, Mr. Cy?"

"I wish I were. A woman in a bikini was fished out of Derek and Annabelle's pool."

"But they've been gone. And the woman who was staying there wouldn't look good in a bikini. Besides, that couple left a few days ago."

"Did you go over to check and see if they left a body behind?"

Joey laughed.

"You're kidding aren't you, Mr. Cy. They didn't look like the type who would do that. I went over to talk to them a couple of times, and the woman even baked some cookies for me. And fixed me ice cream to eat with them. A big bowl of ice cream. A woman like that wouldn't murder someone."

"Sometimes they do. What day did they leave?"

"I think it was Saturday. And Derek and Annabelle came back today. Not long ago. I heard them pull in. I went out and waved to them when they were unloading. Then I came back here to play. I was up in the tree discovering far-off places."

"But you weren't doing any good at discovering bodies in nearby places? Did you see or hear anyone at the house at any time between when the couple left and today?"

"In a way."

"What do you mean by 'in a way'?"

"You know I sleep with my window open sometimes. One night, I heard a car door close. It was late. Nobody on this street comes home late. Well, not since you started sleeping out in the woods with the bears. So, I hopped up out of bed and hurried over to the window. I saw some woman standing in front of Derek and Annabelle's house, looking at it, and the car that must have dropped her off had gone up to the end and turned around and was coming back real slow. Then, whoever it was, drove down the street a couple of more houses and stopped. Whoever it was didn't get out. They just sat there. I turned around to see where the woman was, but she had disappeared. I turned back and looked at the car, but whoever it was wasn't in any hurry to get out or drive off."

"Would you recognize the woman if you saw her again?"

"No. It was too dark. But I'm pretty sure she was young. Do you think she might be the woman in the bikini?"

"Was the woman you saw wearing a bikini?"

Joey laughed again.

"No. She had clothes on."

"Can you tell me anything about the car or the driver?"

"It was a dark car. I couldn't see who was driving it. I guess I should've been paying more attention. But I was still half asleep."

"Is there anything else you can tell me?"

"Just that I think the car might be the same car that drove down the street once or twice when that other couple was staying over there. You think someone left a body there?"

"Or murdered someone there."

"This is turning into a high-crime area. Do you think I should get a gun, Mr. Cy?"

"I think we should wait a while on that. We're not even sure yet that she was murdered."

"So, there were no gunshot wounds?"

"Too noisy with an ace detective across the street. They had to do it quietly. If she was murdered, she was probably drowned."

"Oh."

"Well, we'd better be going. Keep your eyes open, Joey, just in case whoever did it comes back."

Although Joey is getting bigger, he still let the women hug him, and Lou and I give him a high five.

+++

I walked across the street to the house where I made a lot of memories. Ones where I used to have to run into the house as quickly as I could to avoid a former next-door neighbor who wanted to get her claws into me. One where I found a couple of bodies out back. One where I had to go to the hospital and came home in a wheelchair and my wheelchair crashed into a tree in the yard of the house on the other side of me. And the time the wheelchair turned over and I was lying on my back in the rain and Joey came over to ask me what I was doing. And the ones where I figured out who murdered whom.

We spent a few minutes at my old house. I went out to the driveway and visited with Lightning, my yellow VW bug. I could tell she missed me. I missed her too and told her so. I think she was never the same again after the telephone pole fell on her and the bull ran into her. From time to time, I think about taking her out to the house in the woods. I wonder if I should do that. I wonder if I did that if she would miss the old homestead too much.

I thought about driving by Lou's old apartment, but we didn't because I knew those old women in his apartment building would hug him and offer him goodies, and I wasn't sure if Thelma Lou would feel bad because she hadn't baked anything for him that day. The old women who live in the apartment building where Lou still rents an apartment seem to bake every day. At least, they always have something for Lou, every time we drop by unexpectedly.

+++

As we headed back to the woods, I posed a question to the others.

"Do any of you have any ideas?"

I was sure that Jennifer would say Annabelle did it. She was the first one to speak.

"I think it was murder, which is good, because it will give me a chance to solve it before you do, Cy."

"Well, hon, I hope it's simply drowning, because I want to stay home and have you all to myself."

"I think I like your idea better, Cy," my wife said.

"I guess we'll cool our heels until Frank calls and lets us know whether it was murder or not. If it was, I will find out the best Frank can tell me about when it happened. Maybe I can eliminate the two couples who have spent multiple nights in that house recently. I will also call North Carolina, find out who has jurisdiction regarding that death, and find out if that woman was murdered. If so, maybe we can compare notes to see if the same person has been traveling and committed both murders. I would think it would be too much of a coincidence to think it was two different people unless they were working together."

I was thinking about what Joey said. If whomever he saw that night was driving the same car that had driven down the street earlier, then whomever it was was determined to dump a body in that particular pool. If that was the case, why deposit it at Derek and Annabelle's house? I decided not to worry about it until Frank tells me it was murder. In other words, I was pretty sure I would be worrying soon.

+++

Lou must not have been feeling well because he behaved himself on the way home. He didn't open his mouth until we got back to the old homestead.

"Cy, it's a good thing that you don't live at your old house anymore."

"Why is that, Lou?"

"Because you would be mowing your lawn."

"Lou, you know that Mark, the yard boy, mowed my grass and shoveled my snow. Of course, he's grown up and off to college now and his younger brother does it. By the way, I forgot to tell you, I heard from him the other day. That girl he brought to the house one day, the one who shoveled more snow than he did, well, the two of them are engaged. They plan to be married after they graduate. I don't guess you did any of the mowing back at your apartment building. You let those little old ladies do all of it. Right?"

"Of course. And bring me some cold lemonade when I got too hot watching them mow."

We both laughed. We both knew the owner paid someone to mow it regularly.

+++

When we pulled into the drive, we figured we had had enough of each other and parted ways. Well, not totally. Jennifer and I hadn't had enough of each other. We headed to our house and Lou and Thelma Lou headed to theirs.

I walked in the door and realized that I had nothing to do until Frank called. I had time to watch all three *Godfather* movies, *Gone With the Wind, The Sound of Music, West Side Story, How The West Was Won, Titanic,* and *The Bridge on the River Kwai* before I would find out if Jane Doe was murdered. The only problem was that I had already watched all of them in the last few months. So, I plopped down and took a nap. Well, after Jennifer felt I needed some lunch.

6

The rest of the day was uneventful. We did what God did after He created the earth. We rested.

I was half asleep and half awake the next morning thinking about what Jennifer and I had done just a few days before.

The sun was shining bright on my old Kentucky home. Jennifer and I started out sitting a spell on our front porch (as the old folks might say), sat there a while before moving to the back deck, and then got up and walked through the meadow and then into the woods. We walked through the field, felt the breeze, and saw it blowing through the meadow grass to our left and the trees off to our right. We strolled. We lingered. We stopped and enjoyed the view. We didn't see any scampering animals off in the distance. But we were looking in the wrong direction.

We had gone several hundred feet from the house before we realized that we were not alone. No, not the other newlyweds. It was a dog and a duck. Our dog and our duck. And the duck seemed to be laughing like they had pulled a fast one on us. But Quiggley refrained from flying up onto my shoulder, and Blue didn't jump up on Jennifer or roll over on his back to get her to rub his tummy. They knew it was a serious moment for us. So, they kept their distance and did not follow us when we slipped off into the woods. They knew we would return the same way at some point.

After several minutes of quiet reflection, Jennifer broke the silence.

"Cy, are you thankful that you can do anything you want?"

"Well, I'm still having trouble juggling those bowling balls. I broke my foot twice."

"Get serious."

"Every morning. And thankful that I have someone to do it with. Well, anything except getting up out of my chair on the first try. That seems to be harder to do with each passing year. And trying to remember what I went into the kitchen to get. I'm almost sixty, you know."

"And I'm knocking on fifty's door. But when did you ever go into the kitchen to get anything? I always get it for you. Besides, I know you can still get up out of your chair with no problem and your memory is still fine."

"I'm thankful for what you do for me too. But turning more serious. As you know, I got married for the first time expecting to be married forever. Forever didn't last all that long. Cancer intervened. That was over twenty-five years ago. We can't live our lives as if we have forever to live them. We need to enjoy each day and thank God for it. Not waste them. It's okay to sit around and do nothing, as long as nothing is what we want to do that day. And sitting on the front porch or back deck is not doing 'nothing'. It's enjoying a small part of God's creation. Let's make it a point to enjoy however much life we have left."

"I agree. But there are times I need to be by myself."

"I know. Women are that way. But I hope there aren't too many of those days."

"Not when I have you."

"I also don't understand why women go shopping, while men go buying. And why do women buy clothes that button up the back? Men don't do that."

She laughed.

"Not as many women do anymore. Cy, I look old to me. Do I look old to you?"

I was smart enough to know how to answer that question.

"Of course not. You are not old."

We grew quiet again and looked around at the familiar and the not-so-familiar. We walked up to where another murder victim had lived and looked and saw the cabins of some of the people I had questioned about that murder. We walked through the woods, careful where we stepped. Although we seldom saw a snake when we were out, that didn't mean there weren't any there.

Eventually, my bones began to tire, and my body began to sweat. Jennifer, on the other hand, had more energy, but I did see a glow about her. I would never call perspiration on a woman sweat. After a while, we headed toward the house. As we came out of the woods, there were two lazy animals there to greet us. They pretended to be happy to see us again. I knew they were sucking up to us to give them some kind of treat when we returned to the house. I was sure they would pay more attention to Jennifer when we got back, and she was assuredly the one who would provide a greater treat.

When we made it back to the house, I walked in and through the house to the front porch. I knew where the shade was. Once Jennifer had provided the two actors with a buffet, she joined me on the porch. I must have looked pathetic too because she brought me a cold glass of lemonade and something to munch on. And that's when we sat down and talked about the things we wanted to do. None of them involved solving a murder. Thinking about that must have triggered something in Frank's brain, because the phone rang, jarring me wide awake. Jennifer came to the door and told me the call was for me. I got up and stumbled to the phone.

"Good morning, Cy."

Even though we had been engaging in vigorous exercise, it wasn't yet noon, so it was still morning.

"It's about time, Frank. I was beginning to think you had gone on vacation, or the woman you fished out of the pool was Mrs. Lazarus."

"I knew he had a couple of sisters, Mary and Martha, I believe it was. But I didn't realize he had a wife. What was her name?"

"Just tell me the name of the woman you found in the pool, and if she was murdered."

"She was unable to tell me her name, but she was murdered, and she was murdered where she was found. She was drowned, and whoever held his or her hands around her neck helped her stay underwater long enough to drown her."

"Is there anything else you can tell me?"

"Just that I'm through with her. It's your turn now. I'll let you contact her next of kin."

I ignored his comment and asked him another question.

"Did you by any chance talk to the medical examiner or coroner down in North Carolina to find out about the person who died down there?"

"There were too many who died down there for me to find out about any of them. Maybe you can see what you can find out. Try to limit the bodies you send me to one per decade from now on."

"I'll do my best."

I hung up the phone, unsure what to do next. I thought for a moment, then called Lou and told him I was going to try to find out about the dead person in North Carolina. I was surprised his response wasn't a joke. I needed to call Derek and Annabelle first to find out where I was to start and to let them know that the person who died in their pool, definitely died in their pool and that someone else helped them die. Then I needed to find out the names of the couple who owned the place where they stayed, and the address of that house. That would give me a place to start. Maybe I would check with Sam to do some of my work for me. I know how much he loves doing it.

And so, that was how my Thursday morning started. And it started early. Which is good, because I now have a lot to do.

+++

I called Derek and Annabelle. My luck was bad. Derek answered.

"Derek, this is Cy. Bad news. Our medical examiner called. The woman in your pool was murdered, and she was murdered at your house. Someone drowned her. We don't know who she was yet. Joey saw a dark-color car over at your house one night after the other couple left. A woman got out and whoever was driving the car pulled down a couple of houses and stopped. By the time Joey looked back at the woman she was gone. I don't know if she went to your house or somewhere else. We don't know who the driver was. Do you have any idea who this might have been? Do any of your friends drive a dark car, possibly a gray or black one?"

"Lots of people drive dark cars, especially gray ones. I'm sure I know some of them. But I don't have a clue about any of this, Cy."

"Then give me the name and phone number of the couple who stayed at your house. I want to find out what happened in North Carolina to see if there might be a connection."

Derek gave me the information I sought, and I made a second phone call. A man answered there, too.

+++

"Is this Howard Higginbotham?"
"It is. Who's this?"

"I'm Lt. Dekker, a homicide detective in Hilldale, Kentucky. I'm calling about a body found at your house. I want to know what you can tell me about it, and the name of the detective who came to talk to you. I need to contact him."

"As you probably already know, my wife and I just got back from a home swap in your town. We left there on Saturday and took our time getting home. We didn't get home until Wednesday. We didn't know we were coming home to a dead body. We walked in the door with some luggage and received quite a fright. A man was lying on our couch. At first, we thought it was a burglar or a drunk who broke in and fell asleep. We called the police immediately. We waited outside and didn't know he had been murdered until after the police arrived. We should have known by the smell, but we didn't. We were tired and weren't thinking straight. Another strange thing was that he had a book written by the couple up your way whose house we stayed in tucked under his arm."

"Derek and Annabelle Oxley."

"That's them. I assume you are familiar with them."

"They used to be my next-door neighbors. I still own the house next door to where you stayed, but I now live in a house out in the woods. Did the police question you about the man you found? Did you recognize him?"

"They asked. I never saw him before."

"Do you by any chance own a dark-color car?"

"We have a gray Mercedes, but it was our red Escalade that we drove to Kentucky. Why do you ask?"

"A neighbor saw one on the street while you were here. It wasn't anyone who lives on the street. Did you see one while you were here?"

"I didn't. If my wife saw one, either she didn't think anything about it or it didn't seem suspicious."

"Why did it take you so long to get home after you left Hilldale?"

"We stayed a couple of days in West Virginia and one in Virginia on the way home."

"I guess you have proof of this."

"Oh, yes. The Greenbrier is a most delightful place."

"I know. My wife and I stayed there on our honeymoon."

"Just curious, but did you see the name of the book the dead man was holding?"

"I did. It was *Bad Swap*. I don't know if whoever killed him left it on purpose, or if it was merely a coincidence. It wasn't anything from our collection. Although, we did look through some of the Oxleys' books while we were at their house, and I think we are going to give their books a try."

"And what is your wife's name?"

"Gwen."

"Can you give me the name and contact information of the detective who came to see you?"

"Just a second. I laid his card on the bookshelf."

He came back a few seconds later and I wrote down the detective's name and number, then told him I would call him back if I had any further questions.

+++

"Detective Dinwiddie."

"This is Lt. Dekker in Kentucky. I'm calling you about a body you found at Howard Higginbotham's house."

"That is quite a mouthful, isn't it, Lieutenant?"

"It is, and you can call me Cy."

"Fine. Call me Jim. What do you need to know? And why are you interested in a murder in our jurisdiction? Don't you have enough happening in your neck of the woods?"

"I'm retired when no one is murdered, so one body is too many for me. But it just so happens that the Higginbothams and the Oxleys were involved in a home swap, and a body was found in both houses. Our body was cleaner. It was found in a swimming pool."

"Ours smelled worse. Oxleys, huh? You think the two murders might be related. Do you know that our guy was found with a book written by the Oxleys in the crook of his arm?"

"I just found that out from Higginbotham. And if both of them are telling the truth about where they were, and I know the Oxleys personally and think they are telling the truth, then neither of them could have committed either murder. So, it seems like someone has it in for both of them. And, according to the Oxleys, they have never met the Higginbothams. Tell me about your guy and when and where he was murdered."

"He was hit over the head and brought here. He was murdered before he arrived here. He was a young man. We have no idea who he was. Nothing has turned up so far in a fingerprint search. Now tell me about your guy."

"Our guy looked good in a bikini."

"So, yours wasn't a guy?"

"No, a young, good-looking woman."

"Do you think they knew each other?"

"Could have been husband and wife. I have no idea. And we don't know where they were from, so we don't know where to check Missing Persons. Any observations about your guy?"

"This is strictly conjecture, but my guess is he was fairly well off."

"But he didn't have any identification on him?"

"Nothing. But his clothes and shoes looked well-to-do."

"And neither couple knew either victim. How long had he been dead when you arrived?"

"Not long. Probably between a day and two days."

"So, if the same person or persons murdered both people, the murder in Hilldale probably happened first. I'll check Facebook and Twitter and see if the Oxleys and the

Higginbothams knew any of the same couples, and if we are lucky enough to find a picture, we will see if the pictures look anything like either victim. Can you send me a picture of your victim and I'll send you one of mine?"

"Will do, Cy."

"Let's keep in touch, and if you're up our way, look me up. Especially if you're not interested in working."

I heard him laughing as he hung up.

+++

I hung up the phone and called Lou.

"I hope I didn't wake you."

"You must have been working for a change, Cy."

"I have been, and it's not a change I like. I talked to Derek, Howard Higginbotham, and Jim Dinwiddie."

"Howard who?"

"You remember Howard, don't you?"

"Howard the Duck?"

"Don't you remember? The duck's name is Quiggley."

"Quigley Down Under?"

"I don't know where Quiggley is now."

"Okay. Who are those last two guys?"

"Howard Higginbotham and his wife Gwen stayed in Derek and Annabelle's house for a week, and Jim Dinwiddie is the detective in North Carolina who went to check out the body found in their house."

"A woman found in a bikini in their pool?"

"Wrong on all counts."

"So, it was a man."

"How did you come up with that so quickly, Lou? And without any clues."

"Out with it, Cy."

"Okay, it was a young man, fully and finely dressed, according to Detective Dinwiddie. He was found on the couch. And guess what he was holding under his arm?"

"A baby."

"Nope."

"A woman in a bikini."

"Guess again."

"The killer."

"Maybe I should just tell you. A copy of a book called *Bad Swap*. Do you know who wrote the book?"

"Obviously you didn't, and I didn't, so I'm guessing Derek and Annabelle."

"Your guessing is getting better."

"They're the only authors I know personally."

"You don't know John, Paul, Peter, and Jeremiah?"

"You have your groups mixed up, Cy. It was John, Paul, Ringo, and George. And Peter is with Paul and Mary. And Jeremiah was a bullfrog."

"I know. He was a good friend of mine. By the way, what is today's clue?"

"How are they all connected?"

"That seems pretty straightforward. I assume we are talking about Derek and Annabelle, Howard and Gwen Higginbotham, the victims, and the murderer or murderers. Seems simple enough. Let me know when you figure it out, Lou."

"Shouldn't we just sit back and let the girls do it?"

"We could, but then we would never hear the end of it from them, and George and Frank. We'll have to get involved too. Of course, we could always let them do all the work and then jump in at the end."

"Does this mean we have to go to North Carolina, too?"

"I hope not. I'll be sure to let Frank know that he didn't have to autopsy that body too. It smelled a lot."

"And he doesn't have to say Harry Higginbotham a thousand times."

"It's Howard, Lou. Not Harry."

"So, it could've been worse."

"It's time to get to work. Maybe the book the dead guy was holding is a clue. I'm going to check Facebook to see if the two couples have any friends in common. You check Twitter."

"Why do I have to check Twitter? Twitter sounds harder."

"It is. That's why I'm giving it to you. You know more about electronic stuff."

+++

I hung up from talking to Lou and called my man Sam.

"This is Sam I Am, I'm not dining on anything at the moment. Is this the guy who used to get lucky and solve murders before he got married?"

"I solved a couple of murders after I married Jennifer, I'll have you know."

"I thought the Mrs. solved that one."

"Nope. It was me."

"So, what do you want this time? Does it have anything to do with that body that was found next door to your house in town?"

"No. It has to do with a body found in North Carolina."

"Always a wise guy."

"Actually, it does have to do with a body found in North Carolina. Find out what you can about a man named Howard Higginbotham."

"Are you serious about that name or are you playing games again?"

"I'm serious."

"He should change his name. Is he the guy who died?"

"No, he is the guy who swapped his home for the one where the body was found here. There was one found in his home in North Carolina too. I want to know where he was between when he said he was here and when he said he got home on Wednesday. Did he really go to Greenbrier in West Virginia? Find out anything that can document where he was. We want to make sure he didn't kill either person. And if you can tell me who the two dead people are, that would be better. I will let Jennifer kiss you."

"On the lips?"

"We'll see."

"You can do the same thing about Derek and Annabelle, but I can't see them killing anyone."

"Can she kiss me, too?"

"Well, she kissed me."

"Was she sanitized afterward?"

"Never mind. I don't think she would lower herself to kiss you."

"I didn't realize she was that tall."

I groaned as I heard that one.

"Do you have twelve more people for me to check on?"

"I'm not sure if Joey, across the street, has an alibi. So, if you want to check on him too, feel free to do so."

"Goodbye, Cy. I have to get off here before I lose my appetite."

7

I had one more call to make. Derek and Annabelle again. My luck was still no good. Derek answered again.

"Derek, Cy again. How much do you know about the North Carolina murder?"

"Not much. Some guy was murdered. The Higginbothams found him on the couch."

"Then you know about as much as I do."

"But only because they found their dead guy before Annabelle found that woman in our pool. Do you know any more, Cy?"

"Not yet. I'm working on the murder here, and Detective Dinwiddie is working on the one down there. We're trying to find out if they are connected. It sure seems like they have to be. I'll let you know if I need anything else."

"Okay, Cy. We're trying to be safe here. We've checked, and we can't find anything missing from the house. It doesn't seem like a robbery. I hope you're not as confused as I am."

I wasn't going to tell him that I was, so I said goodbye and hung up. I was still using my old landline. I only use my cell phone when I'm away from the house. I still don't like using those things.

+++

I headed to my computer. A desktop. I wanted to consult Facebook to see if I could find out who the dead people were and if they knew each other. I had planned to do that earlier but hadn't gotten around to it.

I opened up Facebook and saw that I had a friend request from someone Jennifer wouldn't want me to be friends with. I doubted if the person who sent me the request matched the picture that stared back at me. I wasn't about to find out. I wondered if Lou got a similar request. But I only wondered for a moment. It was time to get to work.

Detective Dinwiddie had sent me a picture of the guy who wouldn't be sleeping on any more couches. He was no one I had ever seen. I put it beside the picture of the woman who was found dead in the Oxleys' pool. I could see where they might go for each other. But my job wasn't to make a love connection. Besides, it was a little late for that.

I wasn't sure if it was good or bad that neither Derek nor Annabelle had many Facebook friends. I knew that it was bad that neither of them had one that looked like either of the pictures that were in front of me. At least they hadn't lied to me about that.

My next job was to see if I could find a Facebook page for Howard Higginbotham and Gwen Higginbotham. I couldn't find one for him, but she had one. I looked through her friends. He wasn't one of them. Either the two of them shared their thoughts privately, or he wasn't on Facebook. I already knew that she wasn't Facebook friends with either Derek or Annabelle, but if my memory was as good as I thought it was, they didn't have any friends in common. I was about to try to decide what to do next when the phone rang. I was hoping it was the murderer wanting to confess. It wasn't. At least, I didn't think it was.

+++

I got an idea. I called Scene of the Crime Bookstore to see if they had a couple of copies of *Bad Swap* by Derek and Annabelle Oxley. They did. I told them to hold them, and that I might be in to pick them up. Then I called Lou.

"Hey, good buddy."

"I'm not interested."

"You're not interested in what?"

"I'm not interested in anything that starts "Hey, good buddy."

"This isn't anything bad."

"Tell me, and I'll decide if it's bad or not."

"Reading."

"I need more information than that."

"The dead guy in North Carolina had a copy of *Bad Swap* tucked under his arm when he was found."

"I'm not going to North Carolina to pick it up."

"How about the Scene Of The Crime Bookstore?"

"They picked up the book?"

"No, Derek and Annabelle sold more than one copy, and if you're willing to go to town with me, they'll sell a couple more copies."

"You think they wrote the name of the killer in there?"

"Maybe they wrote something in there that gave the killer ideas."

"Why don't we talk to Derek and Annabelle instead?"

"Fine. You talk to Derek and I'll talk to Annabelle."

"And I'll talk to Jennifer."

"Just get your shoes on and meet me at the van. And bring some money. I'm not paying for your copy."

I told Jennifer what we were doing. She must have believed me because she didn't follow me.

We got to town and didn't waste any time perusing the shelves. This was a working trip, not a pleasure one. I got back home, kicked my shoes off, and got ready to read. Before I could, the phone rang. My phone had been ringing too often to suit me.

+++

"I wish all of your jobs were this easy. I didn't even have to miss a meal."

"I don't think you've missed too many meals, Sam. You have something for me?"

"No. I just wanted to wake you. Of course, I have something for you. For a change, I think you'll like the idea that you have to keep working. Both couples were where they said they were when they said they were. They were even at that place in West Virginia on the same night."

"Maybe they were shifting the body from one car to the other."

"I don't think so, Cy. Everything works out the way both medical examiners said. Neither of these couples could have murdered either party. You're going to have to look elsewhere for your murderer. I know you're happy about that as far as one couple is concerned."

"Well, one half of one couple anyway. Thanks for getting back to me quickly. I'll try to shoot some more business your way."

"Don't try too hard."

+++

Before I could get back to my chair, the phone rang again.

"Cy, this is Derek. I hope I'm not interrupting you, but Annabelle has an idea."

If Annabelle has an idea, it's okay to interrupt me. I was glad that Jennifer couldn't read my innermost thoughts. Or could she? She came into the room at that moment.

"Cy, we'd like for you to come over. Annabelle has an idea about how you might be able to catch the murderer, and you might have some fun too."

I was wondering if Annabelle shared her idea with Derek.

"Uh, I guess I can do it. Now?"

"Now would be great."

"Okay. I'll see you in about a half hour."

"Who was that, Cy? Whom will you see in a half hour?"

"Derek. Uh, he has an idea that might help me catch the murderer and wants me to come over so he can share it with me."

"Are you sure it wasn't Annabelle?"

"It sure sounded like Derek. But I think she will be there too."

"I think I'll go with you, in case Derek has to go out to pick up lunch and their mail."

"Okay. We might as well invite the neighbors too."

"I guess a half hour will give Annabelle enough time to put her bikini on."

"I don't think she wears it all the time."

"But you'll manage to pay attention to her, Cy."

"I'm sure I will. Derek said it was her idea."

"So, she was the one who wants you to come over?"

"No, she is the one who came up with the idea of how to catch the murderer. Derek said it should be a lot of fun too."

"For whom?"

"Me. And you too if you are involved."

"I'll be involved."

+++

I called Lou and told him we were off to Derek and Annabelle's to have fun. If I had told him that we were going to find out how to catch a murderer, he might not have been as eager to go.

Our neighbors came running out of their house and met us at the van. Lou seemed more eager for this trip than the last one. I backed out of the driveway onto the road that no one uses except us. Before I could head forward, Lou did what he considers his job. He turned the radio on. They were playing *Fifty Ways To Leave Your Lover*. Jennifer was sitting in the middle seat with Thelma Lou. I caught her eye. I gave her the look that said, I didn't pick the song. The next one was *She Loves You*. I tried to convey to Jennifer that it must be her. She gave me the look that she wasn't sure that the song didn't refer to Annabelle. My silent communication let her know that Annabelle wasn't born when the Beatles sang that song. The look she gave me back said Annabelle was born when the century changed, which wasn't true but wasn't far wrong.

Lou's communication was verbal.

"Cy, you missed the turnoff. Watch where you are going!"

"I was distracted by Jennifer's gorgeous looks."

Jennifer gave a look back that said she wasn't buying that.

8

We arrived at Derek and Annabelle's and Annabelle greeted us at the door. She wasn't wearing a bikini. The shorts she was wearing covered slightly more, although I'm sure she wasn't aware of what she had on. She gave me a big hug which ended when Jennifer slithered in to give her one.

As soon as we were seated, Jennifer decided we weren't going to waste any time.

"So, Annabelle, what's this great idea that Cy tells me you have? I can't wait any longer to hear it."

"Well, Derek and I were talking, and I think that the two victims could have something to do with the home swap group we are a part of."

"Why do you think that?"

"Well, one of the victims was found here, and the other one was found at the home of the couple who was staying here."

"But couldn't it just be someone who has something against you? After all, one of your books was found in the arm of the victim that was found in the house where you stayed."

Annabelle hesitated, certainly bothered by Jennifer's comment.

"I guess that could be the case. But Derek and I came up with an idea that could be fun and could lead you, Cy, (she turned to face me as she said this) to apprehend the murderer. For the first time, as far as I know, the home swap group that Derek and I are a part of is getting together next week. We have never met any of the others because even though we have stayed in some of their homes, we are usually on the road going to their place when they are on the road coming to ours. This will give us a chance to meet some of the people whose homes we have stayed in. Also, people who are considering becoming a part of the home swap group can be a part of the weekend and check it out to see if they would like to be a part of the group. There will be a group session talking about what a home swap is like, and then some people will talk about their experiences and what swapping homes for a week or two has meant to them. We thought maybe the four of you would like to go and see if any of these people can identify your victims, or if you think any of them might have murdered one or both of them. You might even like the idea enough that you might want to do what we do. You can do it as much as you like, provided someone else is interested in your home and you are interested in theirs."

"Where is this going to take place?"

"At a hotel in the Catskills. It's an expensive place. Mohonk Mountain House."

"A whole bunch of people will be staying in one house?"

"No. It was a castle at one time. It's in the Catskills and next to the water. They have rooms and suites. I hear the food is great. We're looking forward to it, and to meeting some of the other people and finding out about places we don't know about yet."

"And we can go and pretend that we are interested?"

"You might want to try it. You can always drop out if you don't like it."

"But we don't own the house in the woods. Not yet anyway. And I doubt if anyone is interested in our house next door here."

"You wouldn't think someone would be interested in this one, would you? Considering it is a small house. At least by some people's standards. Of course, we have added on and put in a pool. But sometimes people who live in a large house want to try something different for a week or two. Or try a different part of the country without staying in a motel or a bed-and-breakfast. And even in this small house, we do have something to offer them. We now have a pool and a hot tub. We have a library that not only has our books but a lot of other authors as well. Some people like curling up and reading for a week or two. And then we have our game room. You've seen it. It's got a pool table, a ping pong table, a couple of pinball machines, and a few other game machines. Some people like that and all of this is a big draw for someone who has teenagers. And we still have two bedrooms left over. If someone needs more than that, they can bring sleeping bags. This place isn't for everyone, but, as you know, we've found people who have been interested. That's how we've gone away to other places a few times a year."

"I never thought of it that way. You do have something to offer. But my house next door doesn't have that."

"But you have the money to add on to the house and add some of those things. But you don't have to do anything now. Just go, see if you spot any potential suspects, and see what swapping houses offer and if it might ever be something you would ever be interested in."

"We'll think about it. If we do go, it might either give us some suspects or eliminate some. We don't have much to go on right now. We don't even know who the dead people are. They might be home swappers, or they might not.

"When are the two of you leaving?"
"We haven't decided yet."
"Are you driving or flying?"

"Oh, we always drive. That way we get to see more of the country. And if we find a part of the country where we might want to spend some time, we look and see if we see anyone there who might be someone in the group. And sometimes we go on trips where we stay in hotels too. We're not going to make this trip in one day. It's seven hundred and fifty miles."

We visited for a few more minutes. The others asked some questions and then we left. Jennifer was thankful that I didn't ask if I could go swimming with Annabelle. We talked about the idea of the four of us going to the house swap weekend and grilling some suspects. Well, maybe it wouldn't come to that, but it would give us a chance to see the Catskills, an area of the country where we have never been, and to meet some of these people. I wondered if Howard Higginbotham would be there and if he has a brother named Harry. I figured when I got home I had a phone call to make, and I felt I had all the cards in my favor.

+++

We talked about it on the way home and decided to make the trip. We also agreed to leave early and take in some vacation spots on the way up. When we got home, we got our heads together, agreed on two Mountain View suites, and made reservations to check in next Wednesday. Activities begin for the group on Thursday, although a lot of them won't be checking in until Friday. We planned to get together late Friday morning of this week to decide when we will leave and where we will stop on the way up.

+++

"Hello, Chief."

"Cy, are you calling to tell me you have the case solved?"

"No, I'm calling to tell you the four of us are going away."

"Is that you, Jennifer, the dog, and the duck, or you, Jennifer, Lou, and Thelma Lou?"

"The human four."

"You have a lead on the case."

"Possibly."

"And where are you going?"

"To a hotel in the Catskills."

"Cy, is this a lead, a vacation, or a chance to forget the case and get away from me?"

"It's a possible lead and a chance to get away from you."

"Has another body turned up there?"

"Some will in a little over a week."

"And how do you know that?"

"Annabelle told me."

"Is this the Annabelle with the good body who found another good body that was no longer breathing?"

"One and the same."

"Have you considered the fact that she might have murdered the woman she found in her house?"

"No. And Sam has cleared both Annabelle and Derek and the couple who lives in the house they stayed in. All four of them have alibis for the times of the two murders."

"Is this the Sam who works for us?"

"It is."

"Is he infatuated with Annabelle's body?"

"He is, but he too is happily married. And he is not infatuated with any of the other three people he has cleared for both murders. Plus, I have a witness who has cleared all three of them."

"And who is that?"

"Joey."

"Does he work for us too?"

"Sort of."

"What does that mean?"

"He's the little boy who lives across the street from Derek and Annabelle. He does surveillance work for me."

"And is he infatuated with Annabelle too?"

"He's too young for that. But both she and the other female suspect did bake cookies for him."

"Would that cause him to lie?"

"Maybe. Maybe not. It might cause me to lie if it was a charge a lot less than murder."

"I'll have to remember that. So, why do you want to go to the Catskills?"

"Because both of these bodies turned up in the homes of people who do home swaps. There will be a gathering of people who do home swaps there in a little over a week, plus people who are considering doing that, and Annabelle thought maybe the murderer will be there."

"Does that mean we have to put Annabelle on the payroll?"

"I'll ask her."

"Never mind. How long will you be gone?"

"Maybe a week."

"Wouldn't it be better if you went to these people's homes?"

"It might be, but that might take a year."

"And you don't know who either victim is yet?"

"That's right."

"So, you'll be vague when you ask them about murder. You'll ask them if they have murdered anyone at all within the last month."

"I might show them a picture of the two victims and see if they drop what they are eating or drinking."

"Just don't stay any extra days. I wish I could find someone else as good as you are at solving murders."

"Me, too, Chief. Me, too."

+++

Something the Chief said bothered me. I hadn't spent any quality time with Blue or Quiggley the last several days.

I called for Blue to come over to me. Jennifer wasn't in the room, so he complied. He lay down and rolled over so that I would rub his tummy. That reminded me. I needed to spend more alone time with Jennifer. She hadn't rubbed my tummy enough lately.

"Blue old boy, have I ever told you about the birds and the ducks?"

"He looked at me quizzically.

"Never mind. Those who love you are going to be going away again for a few days. You will be going to that place where they pamper you more than Jennifer does."

He smiled. It could be that the only thing that could be better is if Jennifer could go there with him. That wasn't going to happen. She was going to some castle with me.

"Let's go tell Quiggley that she will be on her own."

The two of us walked out the back door. I could tell the duck was distraught. She could hardly hold back the tears as she did the backstroke in the hot tub. She motioned for me to throw her a morsel of food. Instead, I reached my hand over the side and stroked her feathers. I could tell she would rather have had the morsel of food. I prefer it when Jennifer strokes my feathers, but some animals are different. I let her know that the other three of us would be going away and she would have the place to herself. I couldn't tell by her reaction if she had discovered a secret way into the house. We were interrupted by Jennifer, who had come out in her swimsuit and had stepped in to join Quiggley. Jennifer has always looked younger than her years. She can pass for somewhere in her thirties. I can pass for two years younger than almost sixty. I took another look at her. I forgot about the two animals and beat a hasty retreat to find my swim trunks.

I got so excited seeing Jennifer that I stubbed my toe and ended up hopping through the kitchen to the bedroom. I was back as quickly as I could and my graceful dive into the hot tub was enough to cause a duck to fly and a dog to flee. I settled as close to my honey as I could and kissed her on the neck. She responded by dunking me. The water skirmish was on. After a couple of minutes of shenanigans, Jennifer and I settled down and whispered sweet nothings in each other's ears until I remembered I had a book to read. Maybe I could rely on Lou's recollection of what he reads. With that thought, I hopped out of the water, went into the house, dripped water all over the floor, changed clothes, and began to read. When Jennifer walked in with a quizzical look on her face, I let her know the task I had before me.

+++

I settled down and began to read Derek and Annabelle's book. While their books are a series, they don't have recurring characters, so it doesn't matter what order a person reads them. That didn't matter to me anyway. I was concerned about this particular book since it is the one the dead man had curled under his arm when he was found. *Bad Swap*. At least, I had an idea of what the title dealt with. I began to read and read until Jennifer called me to eat. I told her that I thought it was a good book so far and asked if she would like to read it when I finished, in case she came up with something that I missed. She told me she would read it if I wanted her to.

After we ate, I spent a little more time with my wife and then got back to the book. I refrained from calling Lou to see how far along he was in his copy of the book. He had probably read more than I had because he hadn't spent any time frolicking in the hot tub with his wife. I wasn't going to ask if he had spent any time frolicking elsewhere.

About three chapters into the book, a murder took place. Someone who had swapped houses with someone else was found murdered in a house that wasn't theirs.

Maybe someone read the book I was reading and decided to go and do likewise. A few more chapters in, but a few months later, another person who didn't live in the house was found murdered in the same house. So far, that hadn't happened in Hilldale. I thought about warning Derek and Annabelle that this might happen, and then I remembered that they were the ones who wrote the book. So, this book wasn't a carbon copy of what had happened here and in North Carolina. Had I already learned everything I was going to get from the book? I hoped not, although I was enjoying the book. Derek and Annabelle or Derek or Annabelle was or were a good writer or writers. I wasn't sure if they wrote an equal amount for each book or if they would even tell me what each one did for each book. Maybe it varies from book to book.

I am a slow, but thorough reader. I also take short breaks from reading every half hour or hour. That means I had not finished the book by the time Jennifer and I usually go to bed. I had nothing pressing for the next morning, so I figured I would continue reading the book then, and I should be able to finish it by lunchtime. Lou would probably be finished then too, so I would call him and see what he deduced from the book. He would probably tell me he figured out who the murderer we are looking for is, but he won't tell me. He would wait for me to figure it out for myself. Then I remembered that they were coming over anyway to make plans for our trip out of town together.

9

So far, I couldn't even figure out the murderer in Derek and Annabelle's book. So how could I figure out who killed whom in the case I'm working on? And in the two murders in their book, the victims' identities were revealed. I had no idea who the woman was in Frank's drawer at the morgue.

With the murder I was getting paid to work on, I knew who the two couples were who had swapped homes. But there was nothing in the house to identify the bikini-clad woman whom Annabelle found floating in their pool. Maybe if Derek and Annabelle had waited to write their book, they could have made it more complex. But even as it was, I didn't figure out who did it.

I wish my case had been easier. Like the murderer had left some incriminating evidence behind. Like a driver's license with a photo ID. I lay in bed for an hour, struggling with a real murder and one that was only part of someone's vivid imagination. Finally, I managed to go to sleep. I would like to say that I woke up and realized who the murderer was, like when authors wake up with a brilliant idea for the book they are working on, or for their next book. But I didn't even know who the dead people were. Maybe I could find that out in New York. The state, not the city. I'm not sure people can figure out anything in New York City. But then I doubt if anyone else notices.

+++

I woke up Friday morning, lay in bed for a moment, and then realized that I was the only one still in bed. Her highness had already arisen. I sprang from the bed as quickly as someone could who hadn't had the two glasses of water he needed to get all of his body parts moving. That means I was able to get up somewhere between the amount of time that it would take a turtle and the time it would take a snail. Of course, I have never seen a turtle or a snail get out of bed, and I don't want to see either of them in my bed. Only a wife, who manages to do it more gracefully than I can. But then she is several years my junior. And even when she reaches the age where I now find myself, I think she will get out of bed more easily than I do now.

I located the above-mentioned wife just getting out of the shower with a towel wrapped around her. She leaned over and kissed me and called me sleepyhead. I took the fact that she had showered that we were skipping our walk in the woods that day. That was fine with me. I would shower first, then spend time with God. Maybe He would whisper to me the names of the recently deceased.

Even though I spent a couple of extra minutes in the shower, He didn't reveal any names to me, so I read another chapter in my Bible. That didn't work either, so I figured He was trying to teach me patience. That wasn't something that came naturally to me.

I ate an ample breakfast, said hi to the dog and the duck who jumped and flapped for joy because of the greeting, and headed back to the book that was going to tell me the names of the young woman Frank had in cold storage, the man who was stored elsewhere, and whomever it was who decided to end their lives. Before lunch, I had finished reading the book and the only thing I had learned is that Derek and Annabelle can spin a good yarn. Was I going to have to wait until someone somewhere missed the two people whose murders I was trying to solve? Maybe someone did miss them already. I hoped they weren't orphans who lived alone in the woods. Maybe it was just that news travels slowly in some places. It was at that point I realized that my best bet was to meet some people who trade homes for a short time with other people. Unless Lou learned more from reading his copy of the book. Unless someone had read his copy before him and made notes in the margin, it meant we were on our way to meet some new people, learn where they live, and how many people they had killed lately. We were looking for someone who had killed at least two.

+++

I picked up the phone and dialed Lou's number.

"Did I wake you, Cy?"

"I'm the one who called you. What did you think of the book?"

"I wasn't all that excited about Leviticus, and Numbers, and those two Chronicles, but some of the other parts were pretty good."

"Speaking of that book, not everything that happened during Jesus' time made it in the book. Did you hear about the pessimist who saw Jesus walking on water? He said I can't believe in any man who can't swim. But back to the matter at hand. I was talking about the other book, Lou?"

"I'm a man of only one religion."

"And I'm a man with a gun who is nearby."

"Oh, that book. I thought it was pretty good. For a while, I thought it was the butler who did it."

"Lou, there was no butler in the book."

"What book did you read, Cy?"

"The same one you did. Now, out with it."

"You mean you lost your copy?"

"I'm about to lose my patience."

"I didn't realize that you're a doctor now. That cop thing didn't work out."

"I'm on my way over there."

"Oh, *that* book. House swapping sounds too dangerous to me. Too many who do it get killed. The next-door neighbor did it, you know."

"That might be true in your case, Lou. Now, get over here and bring the more intelligent one who lives in your house with you, and we'll talk about taking a trip to New York."

I shouldn't have said that. Lou started singing, "Start spreading the news."

"That reminds me of something, Lou. Everyone I've ever met from New York tells me they are from the city or Upstate New York. I've found out that those Upstate people never live near each other. What they mean is they want you to know that they don't live in the 'City That Never Sleeps', where everyone is crazy, and they aren't about to live there. By the way, the place where we are going is about ninety miles from there. You can even take a train to the city if you want. We aren't going into the city. At least, I'm not. You won't be going either, as long as you behave. If you don't, I'll drive you to the nearest subway that is going downtown."

I messed up again. Lou broke into another song.

"When you are alone and life is making you lonely you can always go, Downtown."

"Look through your house. Find someone named Thelma Lou and send her over here. You can stay home in case a murderer should stop by."

+++

I knew it would take Lou awhile to find his shoes, so I headed to the computer, found Google Maps, and checked out how to get from Hilldale, Kentucky to New Paltz, New York, where Mohonk Mountain House is located. Hilldale is not near an interstate. Surprisingly, the place where we would be staying is only a few miles from one. I saw we had two options for getting there, which I was pretty sure of before I got on the computer. I just wasn't sure where in the state of New York that place is.

I was about to look more closely when I heard the pitter-patter of big feet on my front porch. I hurried to lock the door, but I was too late. Blue blocked my path. He was waiting to be petted and get his tummy rubbed. Thelma Lou complied. Lou always waits until he takes his shoes off and then rubs Blue with his sock feet.

I forgot to tell Jennifer that she was having family over, so she came into the room to see what all the noise was. I told her it was a trip-planning session.

Jennifer, ever the hostess, saw that everyone had something to drink and something to munch on before we could get started. Then Lou fluffed his pillow, and I began.

"We have two things to discuss. Whether we take the northern or southern route and when we leave here."

"So, we might go by way of Key West?"

"You may go by way of Tierra del Fuego, Lou, but the rest of us are going either through West Virginia or Ohio. And we need to decide if we are going early and see some things on the way up since we don't seem to be making any headway on the case, or if it is just an up-and-back trip."

"Let's have a little fun, too, Cy," Jennifer responded.

"Then, I suggest we take the southern route. We can leave in the morning if you girls can get packed. We can do Gettysburg on Sunday, Hershey on Monday, and the Amish country on Tuesday. That will put us at our destination on Wednesday afternoon, and we can get to know the place a little bit and be ready for the first of the 'Meet and Greets' on Thursday afternoon. Not everyone will be there for that. But if a lot of people show up, there's no way we will be able to meet everyone at one time and remember who is who."

"Thanks for giving me such long notice, honey."

"I know you can do great things quickly, babe. That's one of the things I love about you."

I thought of how much this was costing us. I had never stayed at any place so expensive. It is a good thing Lou and I have a lot more money than we used to have. The old me couldn't have afforded to stay one night in this place.

Once we had agreed that we were leaving in the morning, the girls put Jennifer's laptop next to my desktop. That was so they could look at the amenities the place offered while Lou and I looked at all the expensive things on the menu. I didn't recognize what all of it was, but I could tell it was expensive. I could tell what the hamburgers and steaks were. It was some of the other fare that gave me trouble.

"Hey, look, hon, they have a spa!"

"That's great! Lou was hoping they would have one."

Everyone laughed except Lou.

"I see too much on the menu that interests me. Thelma Lou can pretty herself up in the spa while I sneak in an extra meal," Lou interjected.

"Maybe we should check to see if they have a place where you boys can work out."

"Do you think they have recliners?"

+++

We took a break, and the girls whipped up something to eat that wasn't nearly as expensive as what we would find in Upstate New York, as only they can, and we continued to talk about our upcoming trip. They were more concerned about the fun parts of it. Lou and I were hoping we would find a murderer while we were there, be able to arrest him or her, and then decide what to do next. Taking the murderer with us as we toured the area was not one of the possibilities.

+++

The washer and dryer were going full force at both houses while Lou and I loaded up Blue to take him off to his life of luxury. Blue tried to act like he was going to miss us. That was until he remembered how he had been pampered there before, and when he saw a cute Golden Retriever that strolled by as we were getting Blue registered. I noticed he held his head high, didn't pay any attention to me, and didn't roll over on his back or lie down and scratch himself while she was in the room. He was ready for Lou and me to leave so he could get on with his own "Meet and Greet" time. I think he forgot that he wasn't staying in a coed dorm. He ignored me when I told him goodbye, and I told him I would remember that when we came back to pick him up in a month or so. When he saw that all the other dogs had left the area, he rubbed up against my leg. I rubbed behind his ears and then Lou and I left.

"Cy, are you looking forward to this trip?"

"I have mixed emotions. It would be a lot more fun if we didn't have to work while we are there."

"It will seem strange, being at a fancy resort and checking out everyone we see to see if any of them look like a murderer."

"What does a murderer look like, Lou?"

"They come in all shapes and sizes, Cy."

"And their victims come without names."

Lou nodded his head to that one.

10

Saturday morning came early. Too early. But early doesn't seem quite as early when you are leaving on vacation. At least the weather was nice. We didn't have to head out in a driving rainstorm. But it was a vacation of murder-solving. That took some of the fun out of it.

We didn't want to waste time or tire the girls out by having them fix a breakfast feast before we left town, so we stopped at a drive-thru on the way out of town. We decided to do life differently. Taco Bell. I had one of their Breakfast Crunchwraps. It's not something you can eat while you drive, because I would have gotten it all over me, so I pulled over and ate it before we left their parking lot. Crunchwraps I can do in the early morning. Salsa I cannot. But then I can't do salsa anytime.

The first part of our drive was only country roads and a few small towns until we got to Morehead and I-64. There isn't as much traffic on 1-64 East in Kentucky as there is on I-75 North or South. Of course, if we had gone the northern route, we wouldn't have hit the interstate until we got near Cincinnati, and that would have meant a lot of traffic, no matter what day of the week it was. We made good time and were soon in West Virginia. As soon as we crossed the state line, Lou started singing "Country roads, take me home.' Lou is no John Denver. I'm not even sure he is a Tiny Tim. The singer, not the Dickens kid.

Lou stopped singing, then got silly.

"I want to hurry up and get to where we're going. I want to see Washington Irving, Rip Van Winkle, and Ichabod Crane."

"I'm sorry to say that all three of them have passed away, Lou. But we are going within about ten miles of Washington Irving's grave in Sleepy Hollow Cemetery. I can let you off at Suffern. There is a road that will take you almost to Sleepy Hollow, close enough that you can walk. Much of Rip Van Winkle's family is buried there, but I'm not sure if he is or not. The real Ichabod Crane was a friend of Irving's, and he is buried on Staten Island. That would be quite a walk for you from Sleepy Hollow, but you could take a cab through New York City to get there. That would be pricey, but you can afford it."

"So, all three of them were real?"

"All but the author. Authors are not real people. They are made up. And the characters in the books are not like the ones in real life. They are merely people Irving knew. But the Crane in the book resembled the real Crane. You know, a few thousand bites short of a good meal."

My information for Lou kept him from singing. Anything that keeps Lou from singing is good. As I thought that, Lou turned on the radio. Glen Campbell was singing *By The Time I Get To Phoenix*. No one gets to more places than Glen Campbell. None of them were places we were going to get to on this trip.

I drove for a while. We stopped for lunch. I looked around the restaurant where we ate. No one I saw there looked like a murderer on the way to Upstate New York. When we left there, I turned the driving over to Lou. He drove until we stopped for the night in Hagerstown, Maryland. We were tired. It was time to eat supper and rest for the night. We didn't have that much farther to go to reach Gettysburg. Jennifer had already booked us a room at a place there. The drive to Hershey the next morning wouldn't be nearly as bad as the one we had covered that day. We would get there by the time a lot of vacationers were just getting up.

We pulled up to the place where we were staying in Gettysburg, just as someone nearby was getting out of their car. I recognized a Rod Stewart song on their radio. It was one of the few of his I knew. One about a woman. I took a minute to talk to the guy.

"I'm an actor, plus I work some in makeup. I play bit parts and work some to make people look like someone they are not."

"What can you do with my friend Lou here?"

The guy laughed.

"I'm not a miracle worker."

That made me laugh. For some reason, Lou didn't laugh at the same things I did.

I found out the guy was on his way to his next gig. He was taking his time. It was only a day away and he had three days to get there. In other words, it was sort of like what we were doing. But I doubted if he was going to try to find a murderer when he got there. I was glad he didn't ask me what I did. I'm not sure what story I would have told him.

+++

Our three-day excursion turned out to be a good variety of what Pennsylvania has to offer, and we didn't even make it to Philadelphia. Lou cried when I told him he wouldn't get to see the Liberty Bell. He said he wasted the money he spent on Crazy Glue and Gorilla Glue.

Our "vacation" on the way to murder solving will always help me to remember the battlefield of Gettysburg and the sadness behind that event, that Hershey has a lot more than just candy bars, and that we got to see the old and new of Pennsylvania Dutch country. I wonder sometimes if the Pennsylvania Dutch, the Amish, and the Mennonites might have a lot of things more right than some of the rest of us. We enjoyed all three places we visited. I made good choices. But now, it was time to head straight up to New York. I asked Lou if he wanted me to drop him off at the exit to Sleepy Hollow Cemetery, but he said we might check it out on the way back.

I was on the way to find a killer when I got a phone call. I saw who my caller was, so I put it on speaker, so everyone could hear.

"Cy, I tried you at home, but I couldn't reach you. Have you already left on your trip?"

"We just crossed over into New Jersey. Are you calling to tell me that someone confessed?"

"No, but I am calling to tell you whom they can confess to murdering."

"You have an identification on both bodies?"

"That I do. Drake and Amanda Peabody. They lived in Islamorada, Florida."

"Isn't that in the Keys?"

"Very good, Cy. You're up on your Keys."

"I am. There are eighty-eight on a piano, and three to my house. But I'm not telling you where I keep my spare key. I guess you want me to go down to the Keys as soon as we leave the resort in New York? At the department's expense, of course."

"I think you've done enough traveling for now. At least you have a couple of names to go on. And by the way, they are part of that home swap thing you keep talking about."

"Maybe Jennifer and I should check out their house for a week and see if we can find any clues. Maybe the murderer has been there. They could have been kidnapped there and murdered elsewhere."

"Maybe if you don't find the murderer within a month. Besides, George said he's free to check on it."

"George couldn't find the water from the beach. Besides, we should be up here for a month."

"I think you said a weekend. Here it is Wednesday and you are almost there. Just see what you can find up there and then come home."

"Come up and join us, Chief. The rooms are under a thousand a night. Well, some of them are."

"Do they rent by the hour? That's all I can afford."

"It's not that kind of place, Chief."

"I have one other tidbit of information. There was a guy there visiting them a few days before their bodies turned up in Kentucky and North Carolina. His name is Brad Hightower. One of the neighbors said he lives in a castle in Vermont. They said he drove an expensive sports car. They had no idea what kind. It wasn't one they recognized."

"Did the neighbor say whether or not he killed them?"

"I don't think either of them died there. Remember?"

"I don't remember much at my age. Maybe you should replace me."

"Goodbye, Cy. And keep him in line, Jennifer."

"I will, Chief. I definitely will. At least I'll try. You know how difficult a job that is."

"I do. I just thank God I don't have to live with him."

"And I thank Him I have never had to live with you, Chief. Spending one night with Lou was bad enough."

"Hey, why bring me into your lover's quarrel?"

"Jennifer and I aren't quarreling."

"I was talking about you and the Chief."

"I'm hanging up. Just find the murderer, Jennifer. I know Laurel and Hardy are hopeless."

"You're showing your age again, Chief."

+++

With all that transpired afterward, I wondered if anyone remembered the victims' names. If so, I wondered who would be the first of my passengers to respond. I shouldn't have wondered.

"Wasn't there a Peabody in a cartoon series?"

"There was, Lou. I don't think they were related."

"Are these the people who owned the hotel in Memphis? Jennifer asked.

"They might be. I bet their house is a doozy."

"And on the beach," Jennifer added. "We should go to the beach sometime, Cy."

"I'm game, as soon as we solve this murder. Well, at least now we have names to drop at our get-together."

Now I was more excited to get to our destination. I wondered how many people would be at this shindig. If it was only one person I didn't recognize, and he or she was carrying around a copy of *Bad Swap,* I might be able to solve the murder. Especially if he or she tried to hit someone over the head with a corner of the book.

+++

My driving wasn't bad, but all of a sudden, Lou jumped in his seat. It was a good thing he was wearing his seatbelt.

"Did I wake you, Lou?"

"No, God did."

"I didn't hear a voice come down from the heavens."

"That's because He was speaking to me."

"And what was He saying? Be nice to your friends?"

"No. Have your friends be nice to you. Actually, he was giving me the clue of the day."

"Which was?"

"The murderer has no sense of humor."

"Well, I don't think I'm going to like this murderer then."

As I drove, I thought of an idea that I might use to find out if some of the people I meet have a sense of humor. Maybe I can eliminate some of my suspects that way. I call it my elevator list. I guess I can leave Lou on my suspect list. He doesn't have much of a sense of humor.

+++

We stopped for lunch. I took the time to look up Islamorada. It was almost in the middle of the Keys. I think it's the longest of the Keys. Maybe that's what the "morada" part means. I'm not up on my Italian, if it is Italian. I'm not up on any other language either. Well, a little bit of English.

I saw a picture of a house on the beach, surrounded by palm trees. The house was three levels, with a wrap-around porch or deck on one of the levels. I wondered if that might be the Peabodys' house. I wouldn't mind spending a week or two in that house. Too bad the Peabodys wouldn't be spending a lot more weeks in it. That way I wouldn't have to spend time I didn't want to spend finding out who killed them. At least, I was headed somewhere nice. I hoped I wasn't about to be added to someone's hit list by being nosy. I expected a fair amount of people to be there. I doubted if one person or couple will stand out over everyone else. Unless they are very tall.

11

We arrived at the place with an unusual name and checked in. I was glad they hadn't heard back yet on their background check on Lou. It helped that Thelma Lou checked them in. I learned two things upon arriving, both of which pleased me. I didn't have to dress for dinner, and all meals were included in the price of our room. Well, I did have to dress, but I could dress casually. There were a few restrictions, but none of them bothered me.

Lou, on the other hand, not as dignified as I am, jumped when he heard about meals being included in the cost. His landing was not the least bit graceful, and he stumbled until his keeper kept him from falling to the floor. Since he was still a suspect, I didn't want him to get evicted before he saw his suite.

We were each given a lanyard to hang around our neck that gave us the right to murder anyone else who had a lanyard, but no one who didn't. It had two types of homes on it. Neither looked like mine, but I didn't hand it back for a replacement. That's what I get for not sending them a picture of my two homes. I would wear it with pride unless I spotted someone who looked like a murderer.

We were shown to our suites, and they were more than satisfactory. Well, other than the fact that Lou's suite was next to mine. As soon as I saw our suite, I wasn't sure I wanted to leave it. We had a tower suite. The lower level had a formal living room, a full bath, a sleeper sofa, and a balcony. A spiral staircase led up to the master bedroom where the Queen and I would sleep on a king-size bed. We had a choice of a soaking tub, which requires you to take two steps up before you fall in, or a glass shower which did not require any steps up. Not wanting to risk injury, I knew I would stick to the shower. There was another balcony on this level, which gave us a magnificent view of the mountains and the valley. I wondered if someone came in hourly to turn down the bed and leave more mints on the pillows. I just knew it was beautiful. I wondered if I could extend my stay. I tried to do the math to see how long it would take me to run out of my millions. I could stay for a few months at least. The only problem is that I have to spend a certain amount of nights in my house in the woods each year, in order to stay there and keep getting the money every year. But that was only for a few more years. Then the house and all of the money would be mine, I mean Jennifer's.

I wanted to scout out the place to get my bearings. I also wanted to see if anyone was running around with multiple copies of *Bad Swap*. If it was anyone other than Derek, I might tackle them. People were milling about, but I didn't think, "How many people have you murdered this month?" was a good icebreaker. Besides, I wasn't sure if I was looking for one person or two. I ruled out a conga line. I didn't see one anyway. I say all of this "I" stuff, but I was not alone. Her highness was with me. The other couple was looking elsewhere. Lou was probably in his room studying the menu, or the inside of his eyelids.

"Well, darling, where should we go first?"

"Maybe take a stroll down to the water. Do you know the way?"

I didn't, but I asked, and soon we were on our way. I had to watch my step on the way down, which prohibited me from enjoying the view as much as I wanted. Once we arrived at our destination, I didn't have to watch my step, so I gazed out upon the water and looked up at the trees without feeling that I might fall in and drown. The walk back up was a little more difficult. I was getting more exercise than I wanted. I'm sure that made Jennifer happy.

I got to choose our second destination. Since I was tired from doing a lot of the driving, I chose one of the multitude of rockers on the porch. There were a lot more than I had on my balcony at Westgate. Even more than outside of each Cracker Barrel. And they were in a straight line, unlike all the rockers that surround the fountain on The Island in Pigeon Forge.

I sat there and enjoyed the view and didn't fall off my rocker. I thought of all the amenities the resort had to offer. I had no interest in walking all the trails that led this way and that. I didn't want to take advantage of the spa, but Jennifer could if she wanted. I might walk down to the indoor pool, but I doubted if I would put my trunks on and dip my toes in the water. Jennifer had put in our swimwear just in case we decided to take advantage of the pool. But I was there to eat and find a murderer.

A few people occupied some of the other rockers. None of them looked like someone planning their next murder. But would there be a *next* murder? Or had whoever murdered that couple whose names we now know finished with their murdering spree almost before it began? Maybe whomever it was only had something against one couple. Somehow, I doubted that.

When I got tired of sitting, I told Jennifer I wanted to walk around a little bit. I asked her if she wanted a spa treatment. She said she would check with Thelma Lou, and maybe the two of them would book a time during the day the next day if they had slots available before the festivities began. I reminded her that most of our free time was in the morning.

The four of us met up. We switched off to his and her teams. Lou and I were trying to decide what to do when I spotted a guy walking through what would be one of the higher-traffic areas during the weekend. He was carrying two copies of *Bad Swap*. I elbowed Lou and almost knocked him down. He must have been thinking of something else, like what to order at dinner.

"Look!"

Not the most observant guy on the planet, he said, "Look at what?"

I pointed at the guy who carried enough copies of Derek and Annabelle's book for two bodies.

"Not my type."

"Good, because that type usually leaves that book with his victims."

That got his attention and he looked more closely.

The guy had stopped for a minute like he was looking for his next prey. Then he took off again. Lou and I tried to follow him, discreetly.

The guy who might be looking for two victims walked into a shop as if he was looking for the right victim. He came out and then walked into another shop. Finally, he opened a door and stepped outside. He took a turn, and we lost him. But not for long. He stepped up behind us.

"You too have been following me. What gives?"

I had to work on my discreet surveillance before I followed the next person carrying Derek and Annabelle's book.

I stuttered for a moment, coming up with what I was going to say. Lou was polite and let me come up with an excuse.

"I notice you have our friends' book."

"You know them?"

"They're my neighbors."

"You're putting me on."

"Nope. So, why are you carrying their books around?"

"I heard they might be here. I hope they will be willing to sign the book."

"But you have two copies."

"That's right. One is mine. One is my neighbor's. He's not here. He is the one who told me about the book. So, I thought I'd do him a favor and maybe I could get his book signed too."

I was trying to figure out if the guy was lying or not. I couldn't tell.

"Why this book?"

"It's the one I've read. It's the one my neighbor recommended to me. Why all the questions?"

I decided to see how he would react to some information.

"A guy died in North Carolina with this book under his arm."

"Really? It's a thriller all right. But it didn't scare me enough for me to have a heart attack."

"It didn't the other guy either. He was murdered."

"I guess it's a good thing I don't live in North Carolina."

"Neither did the other guy."

"I thought you said he died in North Carolina."

"That's where they found his body. He lived in Florida."

"Oh. Did somebody dump him on the side of the road?"

"Nope. On the side of a couch. In someone's home. Someone who wasn't home. Why are you here anyway?"

"I'm a home swapper. You?"

"I'm checking it out. Guess what the dead guy and the ones who weren't at home were?"

"I'm sure you're going to tell me."

"Home swappers. And the guy's wife was found dead at the home of some other home swappers in another state."

"Are you telling me that someone is killing home swappers?"

"It looks that way."

"Was a copy of this book left with his wife's body too?"

"No."

"You had me scared for a minute."

"You should be. Or maybe not. They think maybe the murderer may be here, with copies of this book."

"Well, I'm not the murderer."

"So, who are you? And where do you live if you don't live in North Carolina?"

"I'm George Harrison, and I live in Kansas."

"I'm sorry the band broke up."

"I'm not that George Harrison."

At that moment, I was glad that Lou didn't know the words to any George Harrison song. But I could tell he was trying to think of some. Maybe he did know one and he was waiting until we parted ways with George before he started singing to me. I knew George sang *My Sweet Lord*. But I don't know the words to it.

"So, why are you carrying the books around?"

"In case I run into them."

"But they will be at the Meet and Greet'."

"But so will everyone else. I want some time to talk to them. You say you know them. What are they like?"

I looked around to make sure Jennifer wasn't nearby.

"They are both nice, but she is a lot better looking than he is. She looks really good in a bikini. I doubt if he does, and I don't want to find out. So, tell me. What kind of work do you do, and are you married?"

"I'm a widower, and you might say I'm self-employed. I'm a motivational speaker. I travel around the country speaking to corporate groups. I work about ten days a month. You don't look like a cop, but you act like one. But you don't do a good job of surveillance. What do you do?"

"I'm retired. So is my next-door neighbor here. Sometimes we do a job for a friend. But mostly we do what our wives tell us to do."

He laughed.

"I couldn't see you being a cop, but you are inquisitive. What did you do before?"

"Now, who's being inquisitive? Let's just say it was something that made us wealthy and leave it at that."

"Well, I've gotta go. I guess I'd better take these books back to the room in case someone else gets nosy."

With that, we parted ways.

I was sorry we did. Lou started singing *My Sweet Lord*. Well, the only three words he knew.

"Lou, you know you can call me Cy. But, if you prefer, Your Excellency sounds fine. I never thought of myself as a Lord or a Duke."

That turned out to be enough to get him to quit singing, which told me he didn't know any other George Harrison song or any other words to that one.

12

We met up with the others we came with. I traded one partner for a much better-looking one. Jennifer and I walked a little. We had made dinner reservations for four. I wanted a nap and shower first, so we headed back to the room. I wondered what the other couple was up to, so I had Jennifer text Thelma Lou. She told me what I expected. Lunkhead was asleep.

+++

The resort had a few options for eating, but the main two were the Main Dining Room and the West Dining Room. I thought maybe the North, South, and East Dining Rooms were captured during the Civil War, but this place wasn't built until a few years after that war. Maybe the Smileys weren't thinking big enough when they built the place. Being from Kentucky, I had my eyes set on eating in the South Dining Room.

I heard the view was fantastic from the Main Dining Room. I wasn't sure if that meant the food was bad, so I decided to eat in the West Dining Room without asking the others what they thought. None of them had eaten there either. We arrived on time. Lou had his shoes on and wasn't wearing a baseball cap. That meant he met the requirements for eating in the West Dining Room. Well, there were other requirements too, like wearing pants and a shirt, but Lou always meets those unless he's stumbling into his hot tub at home. Then he wears trunks.

"Lou, even though the food is included in the price of the room, it doesn't mean you can order one of everything."

"Okay, I won't order any vegetables."

"Maybe I should order for you."

"Maybe you shouldn't. I learned how to read last week."

We were seated and Lou behaved as long as there was a restaurant employee near our table.

We looked at the menu. It was a short one. Well, far shorter than the one at The Cheesecake Factory.

All employees walked away so we could make our decisions undisturbed. They didn't know that Lou was already disturbed. I had already noticed that many of the wait staff had come from other countries, and not necessarily the same countries. I guess everyone from another country cannot get a job being on the other end of a helpline when you call. As for what countries the ones who worked at Mohonk were from, I couldn't tell. I wasn't good at determining accents. Well, I could tell New York, New Jersey, and Boston from L.A. (Lower Alabama). But all of these were from foreign countries, and I don't mean California.

"Look, Cy, they shave their cauliflower here."

"I always shave my cauliflower, Lou. Don't you?"

"Only if I'm taking it to a church potluck. And they must have served drinks in the kitchen last night. Their vegetables are already pickled. And their meats must have gone through rehab. It says here they have been cured."

Lou noticed that the girls were giving him dirty looks. I wasn't sure if they were going to lead him out by his ear or make him choose another table.

The three of us who had manners in public talked. We figured we were to order one starter, one entrée, and one dessert. We decided to order a starter we could share, so we ordered deviled eggs and a charcuterie board, even though the vegetables were pickled, and the meats were cured. Lou and I ordered filets, Jennifer ordered chicken, and Thelma Lou ordered cod. All were delicious. When it came time for dessert, I ordered something that I was glad was translated below. They called it Chocolate Mille Feuille. It was puff pastry, with chocolate, and cherries. Jennifer ordered Burnt Basque Cheesecake with Chantilly cream and blood orange ice cream. It tasted better than it sounded. I know. I ate a couple of bites. Lou went for Apple Tarte Tatin with salted caramel and vanilla ice cream. Thelma Lou chose Tres Leches Cake with mango and exotic fruits. I wouldn't be stealing any of her dessert. I don't like milk and I don't like mango. We were all full when we finished, and it was all delicious. Well, all of us liked what we ate.

We left the dining room, went outside, and found four rockers with our names on them. I made the mistake of asking Lou how much we would have to rock to rock off all the pounds we put on at dinner. I found out something I already knew. Lou was no Bill Haley. And I wasn't going to rock around the clock.

While other ears around didn't keep Lou from singing, they did keep us from discussing why we were there at the resort. After we felt we had digested our food enough that we could walk back to our rooms safely, we got up and did just that.

+++

The four of us held a council in our room.

"What's on the agenda for tomorrow, oh fearless leader?"

It was the first time Jennifer had considered me to be the leader. Well, maybe not the first time, but she didn't give me that distinction unless we were working on a case or choosing a place to eat.

"I don't know the particulars yet, but there are two opportunities to meet people who are home swappers or interested in finding out about it. One of them is after breakfast tomorrow. The other is after dinner. At least, I think that's the way it is. I don't know how it will work, but hopefully, we will have a chance to meet some of the other people at each event. There are two more of them on Friday. Supposedly, each of the four is a little different."

"What if I don't feel comfortable interrogating the people?" Thelma Lou asked.

"Just start by introducing yourself. Maybe they will have some kind of an icebreaker. Stick with Lou if you can and let him do most of the talking unless he gets out of line. If you are by yourself, point out your husband, so that they will know you are married and are there with your husband, so no one will get the wrong idea. Then ask them if they are part of the Home Swap group. Tell them you are here with another couple, checking it out, seeing if you want to be a part of it. Ask them what they like or don't like about it. Ask them where they are from and about their house. Then tell them you are looking for a couple named Drake and Amanda Peabody from Islamorada, Florida. Ask them if they know them or have ever stayed in their house. Mention Derek and Annabelle and the Higginbothams. See what their reaction is. Try to talk to as many couples as you can. We'll compare notes when we get back to our suite."

"Sounds easy enough. Well, it doesn't, but I can try," said Thelma Lou, who isn't quite as outgoing as the other three of us.

13

I already knew something I didn't like about the place where we were staying, but I didn't want to think about it. They quit serving breakfast at 9:30. I was used to eating in Gatlinburg and Pigeon Forge, where they quit serving breakfast at 10:30, 11:00, or later. But such is the life of a homicide detective on a working vacation.

When I leave my house and head to some other place to sleep, that doesn't mean I leave my Bible, devotional books, and God behind. I got up early Thursday morning and stepped out onto the balcony. Luckily, I didn't have to look into the sun. But it was already up. I felt the breeze and smelled my armpits. That meant I knew what my next move was. Evidently, Jennifer's nose wasn't as keen as mine because I felt her wrap her arms around my waist. When I guessed Susie on my first guess as to whom it was, I felt someone trying to help me over the balcony railing and down to the valley well below. We reconciled when I turned and received a passionate kiss. An hour or so later, we walked back inside.

I showered, then headed to my Bible and devotional books. Once I had completed the necessities of the day, it was time to go eat. I called Lou to let him know it was time to leave. He told me the breakfast was delicious, but they had already quit serving. I let him know that telling him that was their way of saying they were kicking him out.

+++

On the way down the hall, I sniffed Lou to make sure he had showered. He and I walked ahead of the women until I felt a hand on my shoulder just before we arrived at the Main Dining Room. The one with the view, and food I had not yet tasted. I turned and saw that Lou also had a hand on his shoulder.

A voice whispered, "Boys, do not be boys."

Some people take all the fun out of things. But then I remembered those who look better than we do have never been a boy. I thanked God for that.

After the girls were seated, Lou and I took our seats. We occupied a table next to a window, of which there were many. Lou and I had the outside seats. Away from the window. Men need to sit on the outside in case a server trips and spills something as they walk by.

Jennifer and Thelma Lou admired the view. Lou and I admired the menu. I could look out the window after I ordered, but before my food arrived.

I saw that a Pastry Basket was available upon request. I planned to request one. The menu said it contained apple cinnamon bread, assorted muffins, and plain and chocolate croissants. I would also order a lobster omelet. McDonald's was out of them the last time I drove through. The lobster omelet came with breakfast potatoes. I wondered how much different they are from lunch potatoes.

Lou, not being as refined as I am, ordered the corned beef hash. But since it was a classy place where we stayed, it came with Hollandaise sauce and chives. I told him the chives wouldn't give him hives. He felt better and decided not to ask them to leave them off.

Jennifer decided not to watch her figure and ordered the cinnamon brioche French toast. Thelma Lou decided on eggs Benedict. No repeats among the quartet this time.

Once we had ordered I followed through on my promise to look at the scenery of the places outside where I wouldn't walk. I didn't get to look very long. The Pastry Basket arrived. It was at that point I told Lou to look at all of the beauty outdoors. He must be getting smarter. He looked at the Pastry Basket instead. Since we were eating at a high-class place, we ate and smacked our lips discreetly. We held up our cloth napkins so no one could see us licking our fingers. We refrained from sticking our napkins into our shirts. It helped that our wives had given us a list of what not to do. We could do all of those things in front of Rosie at the Blue Moon, but not here.

+++

I wasn't sure of the home swap schedule, so I headed to the room where things were to happen and checked the schedule. I was wrong about there being two get-togethers. There would only be one. That meant I had more time to knock on each door and grill everyone. And allow someone to drill me. Five minutes later, I was back with the others.

+++

We continued our after-the-meal ritual and headed for the rockers. Someone was sitting on my rocker from the night before. I decided not to make the person move. Jennifer decided that I wasn't going to sit on the rocker next to the woman who was sitting where I sat the night before. I think Jennifer might have let me if she were forty or fifty years older. We couldn't find four rockers together, but we did find two and two. Jennifer decided to trust me alone with Lou, so she sat with Thelma Lou. I would rather have sat with Jennifer. Or next to the one who had good taste in rockers who sat on the same rocker I sat on the night before. After all, she was by herself and might have been lonely. I could have cheered her up. Or taken her off my suspect list.

+++

I had promised Jennifer that I would go on a hike with her. Besides, it would give me a chance to walk off my delicious breakfast.

We checked out the various trails. I wanted to find one that was short, didn't have a lot of ups and downs, and was the one less traveled in case I wanted to sneak a kiss on the way down or back. We agreed on our selection and took off. I looked back a few times. It seemed funny to go for a walk in the woods and not be followed by a dog and a duck. I knew that Blue was having a grand old time, but I wondered about Quiggley. Had she sneaked into the house? Was she doing the backstroke in my hot tub? Did she remember where I left her food and water in case she didn't want to scavenge?

After we had gone far enough away that no one else was nearby, I turned to Jennifer.

"A penny for your thoughts, my love."

"I was just thinking what a great place this would be if you didn't have to chase down a killer."

"Lou and I met George Harrison earlier. He had two copies of *Bad Swap.*"

"I thought he was dead."

"Not only is he not dead, but he lost his British accent. Even if he is not the murderer, maybe we can wrap this up tonight and not let the Chief know."

"You mean that I'll be the chief investigator?"

She smiled and stopped. I remembered our first kiss and tried to make this one better. I found a smooth rock to sit down on and found out Jennifer's thoughts were of something else than what mine were of.

"Cy, do you know whom you would have married if you hadn't married me?

She wouldn't have believed me if I gave her a hasty "No one," so I took a few moments to think.

"I don't know if I would have married her, but if I hadn't met you, I know of someone I would have dated until I was sure one way or another."

"Oh? And who was that?"

"You remember when I went undercover on all of those blind dates where I met different women at The Cheesecake Factory?"

"You know I do."

"Boy, do I know. You, Lou, Thelma Lou, Frank, and George were all there that night I had my first date."

"I remember her. I think the two of you would have made a perfect couple."

"You know good and well she wasn't the one I'm thinking of."

"So, you're still thinking of her huh?"

"Not until you brought up the subject."

"I didn't bring up The Cheesecake Factory. You did. But I think I know which one you are thinking of. What was her name again? And don't tell me you don't remember?"

"Sarah Jane something or other. She was nice."

"And wasn't there a good-looking cop you met just before you met her? One who hit on you?"

"Did I ever tell you that you have too good of a memory?"

"Would you have dated her?"

"It's not good for one cop to date another one."

"Is that why you never dated Lou?"

"For some reason, I've always preferred women. Let's change places. Was there ever a man you almost married?"

"I don't know about almost, but not long before I met you there was a guy I dated a couple of times who ended up moving away and wanting me to move to the same area he was moving to. He wanted to continue the relationship.

I considered it for about twenty minutes one lonely night. Maybe that's the reason I ended up moving to Hilldale."

"What was his name?"

"Homer Hendley. That was another reason I didn't go with him. He carried ballpoint pens in a pocket protector too. There were ink stains of many colors all over it."

We both laughed.

"Was Thelma Lou ever serious about anyone before she met Lou?"

"No. That's the reason she settled for him. She never met any other guys except the ones she knew in high school. They were all either losers, guys who moved away, or got married before she could make herself known."

"Cy, all of this reminds me of something. Did you really have posters of Jennifer Aniston, Jennifer Garner, Jennifer Lopez, Jennifer Lawrence, and Jennifer Nahas on your ceiling before we married?"

"Who was that last one?"

"Jennifer Nahas."

"I couldn't find her poster. They said it was in such high demand they kept running out of it."

"So you had all of the others?"

"Are you kidding? You know I can't reach my ceiling."

"So you hung them on the wall?"

"A lot of unmarried guys have posters on their walls."

"And another thing. I saw one of the recent places you had visited on our computer was a website that had pictures of forty-nine-year-old Angie Harmon in a bikini."

"That was Lou. He came over to use our computer. He said he needed it for a book report. Is she really forty-nine? She looks almost as good as you."

"Nice try there, and she might be fifty by now. And she could have fallen apart in a year. Some women do, you know."

"Not you, at least not yet. Maybe by the time you are eighty. By the way, I've noticed you've started collecting movies with Hugh Grant and Liam Neeson in them."

"What can I say? I'm trying to watch some foreign films lately."

"I think both of them speak English."

"But they're not Americans."

The rock was starting to get hard, so we got up and continued down the trail. We didn't see anyone else until we got closer to where we began. I didn't trip and fall, even though I did think of Angie Harmon in a bikini a couple of times on the way down. Shouldn't her name be Jennifer?

14

I did my best to enjoy the nature of Upstate New York. It was beautiful. I wondered if Lou was back in his suite taking a nap or off looking for Washington Irving. More than likely, he was walking around and checking out the people to see if any of them look like Ichabod Crane.

After a short walk, we were on our way back. I turned around and saw a guy who was carrying a copy of *Bad Swap*. When he noticed that I saw him, he darted behind some trees and then headed into the woods. I said something about it to Jennifer, but when I backtracked and tried to find him, he was gone. I was certain it wasn't George Harrison. I didn't think it was Paul McCartney either. I wasn't going to spend the rest of the day looking for him, whomever he was. Was he on his way to murder someone? Were Jennifer and I those someones? There wasn't anyone else around. Did he know who I was? Did he know that I had a gun? Maybe he was an innocent guy who just happened to have a copy of the book. Derek and Annabelle have sold a lot of copies of that book. Not all of the people who carried a copy around is a murderer. Maybe less than half of them.

I was thankful that it was a cool morning. Jennifer and I got back to our suite without me working up a sweat. I didn't want to have to take another shower before lunch.

I plopped down on the bed and picked up a pamphlet that showed all of the options we had for enjoying ourselves while we were there. We were free until after dinner when we would have our first get-together with those who wanted to snoop around in other people's homes and possibly leave a body or two. We had some time free the next morning after breakfast and the next afternoon too. I wasn't interested in a spa treatment, but maybe Jennifer and Thelma Lou might enjoy that while Lou and I tried something more dangerous, like a tomahawk throw or archery. I wasn't sure I wanted to go horseback riding, but I didn't think I would fall out of a carriage. Maybe the four of us could do that together. We could walk down to the lake, but we had already done that once. But a lot of those other things didn't interest me.

I mentioned these things to Jennifer, and she called the outlaws who shared our ride to the resort. Within a few minutes, we had booked spa treatments for that afternoon for the girls while Lou and I took in archery. If both Lou and I lived through that experience, then we would get to take the carriage ride I booked for the four of us for the next morning. We could have booked the whole carriage for ourselves for the price of a new recliner (a top-of-the-line one), but we decided to share one with four other people. I was willing to save nine hundred dollars to go on only a forty-five-minute ride and possibly share my carriage with a murderer, instead of going for an hour and a half and possibly having Lou serenade the driver. I'm not a cheapskate. I could have gone on one that was only gone half as long. We were paying more to go to Eagles Cliff instead of Copes Lookout. Who wants to go to Copes Lookout? Anyone can go there.

I wondered if I should tell Jennifer that Lou and I were taking part in the tomahawk throw after we had lunch the next day. Should I suggest they have a second spa treatment? No. They would take that to mean they needed more help. Then I would be the one who would need help.

+++

Time passed quickly. There was a knock at the door. Should I slide down my spiral staircase to see who it is? Jennifer spared me that chore. It turned out to be the Lunkhead and his keeper. My daydreaming caused lunchtime to creep up on me.

+++

Lou and I headed down the hall to lunch. He tried to hold my hand. I smacked him. I considered locating my handcuffs when I got back to the room. Next, he tried to whisper in my ear. I smacked him again. When he saw that no one was around except the four of us, he spoke up, but quietly.

"Cy, you're getting old."

"I know."

"That's not what I mean."

"Then what do you mean?"

"Maybe it's because we are away from home. It's lunchtime and you haven't asked me what today's clue is yet. We'll be back to work before the day is over."

"Okay. Out with it. What's today's clue?"

"Pay careful attention to all the people you talk to. Some of them you won't talk to again. Some of them might look different the next time you see them."

"You mean some of them might go home after tonight? And maybe either today or tomorrow there's a costume party and we weren't told?"

"I didn't get the small print. Only the clue."

"You mean that God is sending you the clues by e-mail now?"

"No. Just thought mail. Same as always."

"Well, I hope that all of the women I talk to are ugly or Jennifer is on the other side of the room because she won't want me to pay close attention to the good-looking ones. Be sure and share this with the girls too."

+++

It was time to eat the only meal I hadn't eaten at Mohonk Mountain House. This might be the only thing Lou and I would have to eat until supper. But then I doubted it. I wanted to make sure we didn't starve. Besides, Lou and I had to have enough energy to shoot a bow and arrow.

Lou and I made it to the dining room without a speech from our keepers. We assumed that meant we didn't have to behave. I told him that we weren't allowed to throw food.

We had adjusted to the program. I would see what was outside after lunch, so I took a look at the lunch menu. Lou looked too. Lou recommended the chicken liver parfait to me. I wondered if anyone ever ordered it. I saw a perfect item for him.

"Look, Lou. They have your favorite. Black quinoa salad."

"I only eat the white."

"But it comes with heirloom beets. Not just regular beets, but heirlooms. And if that isn't enough of a selling point, it has roasted mushrooms. Roasted. And basil yogurt dressing."

"I like my Basil with Rathbone, and I like him already dressed."

This was enough to make me miss the Blue Moon. I knew Rosie wouldn't serve this stuff. I looked to see if any of the starters were something I might eat. The Stacked Curried Chicken Salad didn't sound too bad. It came with grapes and pineapple chips. I wondered if the pineapple chips were Lays. I decided to be brave and ordered the Spinach and Ricotta Ravioli. Lou went for a half-pound burger but asked them to leave off the onion jam. Both of the girls picked the pecan-crusted chicken breast.

+++

We checked our watches. We had forty minutes before Lou and I had to get to where Lou would be a target and I would shoot at him, and the girls would get pampered more than Blue was getting pampered so many miles away.

+++

"Lou, when we get there, there is this thing with big and small circles. You are supposed to stand in front of it. That is how they can tell you are part of the home swap group."

"And I'm supposed to catch anything that comes my way."

"If you can. Did I fail to mention that you will be blindfolded?"

"Cy, should we leave if some guy with a bow and one or more arrows has a thing around his neck with two houses on it?"

"That thing is called a lanyard."

"I know that, Cy. I'm more concerned about what might be sticking in my neck."

"Let me check, Lou. It looks like you got a hickey."

"I don't have a hickey. I just want to let you know we have to be careful, and not just when we are in a room full of those people."

We stopped talking when we got close to the archery range and did indeed see some of those people.

"Hi, I'm Rhonda Stephens. I see you're one of us."

"I'm Cy. This is Lou. We're just here considering it. You might say we're checking things out."

I could tell it wasn't Rhonda's first rodeo when she picked up a bow and arrow, took her time, and put an arrow in the bullseye.

Lou turned to me as if to say, "Told you."

"This is my husband, Nick."

Nick did everything Rhonda did except hit the bullseye. I wasn't sure if that meant I should stick closer to Rhonda or Nick. I remembered that neither victim was murdered with a bow and arrow.

"We're from Kentucky."

"We are too," I said, in a voice that sounded like a teenage boy whose voice was changing. "Do you know Derek and Annabelle Oxley? They're from Kentucky too."

"They're the ones who write the home swap mysteries, aren't they? I drove by their home one time, but I haven't met them."

"What about Howard and Gwen Higginbotham or Drake and Amanda Peabody?"

"Those must be pennames. Or did you just make those names up?"

"No. They're real people. I've talked to Higginbotham on the phone, and I've seen Amanda Peabody. They're all part of the home swap group."

"Can't say that I know them. Maybe I'll meet them this weekend."

+++

Lou was receiving instructions while I was talking to the Stephenses. He must not have been paying attention. His first arrow got tired on the way to the target. I refrained from singing *Another One Bites The Dust*. I refrained because he went before I did. My arrow might give up the ghost before it arrives at the target too.

He was hoping I didn't see his first try. I watched his second one too. He compensated, and I'm sure I heard someone cry out in distress in the woods.

Much too soon, it became my time. My first shot hit the edge of the target, got tired, and fell to the ground. My second was good enough to score some points. I was glad Jennifer wasn't there. I was sure she would have beaten me by quite a bit. I watched some other people do better than I did and some who shot like Lou. After our session was over, and Lou and I realized that we were right in not becoming professional archers, we headed for the great indoors and wondered if we would have been better suited for a spa treatment, if Frank and George never found out about it. Before I do something like that, I'll have to make sure there is no mani-pedi involved. I'm not getting my nails painted, even if they used clear polish. Of course, I didn't want a massage either, and I didn't want to look at Lou getting one. That stuff is for women.

"Lou, I have to hand it to you. If someone had been standing there, that one shot of yours might have scuffed his boot a might. And they say the guy you hit in the woods should be out of intensive care in a few weeks."

"You didn't exactly take someone's heart out, Cy."

"I was aiming for his stomach. A heart is important to a woman, but for a man, it's his stomach."

+++

I remembered what Lou had said earlier about the murderer not having a sense of humor, and since my beloved was somewhere where she couldn't see me, I decided to see if I could find the murderer while the others were occupied.

I noticed one shifty-looking guy, so I shuffled up to him and said, "I just got out yesterday. When did you get out?"

He laughed and said, "A couple of weeks ago, any news about Lucky Eddie?"

"I heard he got out and then got run over by a car."

"That's Lucky Eddie all right. That's how he got caught in the first place. He was part of a heist and didn't see the cop who heard he was going to pull the job that night. And the guy was in plain sight."

I left him and walked up to a woman a few years older than I am and whispered in her ear.

"Does your husband know about us yet?"

"Keep your voice down. That's him right over there."

"That guy. I saw him with a blonde half his age last night."

"We just got here a few minutes ago."

"So did we. This was at some restaurant on the way up."

I looked and saw the guy approaching, so I said goodbye and looked for my next quarry.

I had asked Jennifer to show me how to take pictures before we left home, so I had my next line worked out. I saw a good-looking young woman walk into a shop a few feet away. I followed her in and walked up to her.

I put my arm around her, held my phone out, and took a picture of us together before she could move or say anything.

"I just want to remember the time we spent together, brief as it was."

At first, she looked at me like I was crazy. Then she figured it was a joke, and she put her arms around me and gave me a passionate kiss. I was sure that Jennifer would walk in at that moment. Luckily, she didn't and I lived to see another day. Then she looked at me and said, "I'll be at the pool at midnight if you're interested."

While I stood there stunned, a woman approximately ten years my senior came up to me and took my arm, and said, "Let's go. I know things she hasn't learned yet."

This wasn't going the way I had anticipated. I made an excuse that I had someplace to be. I figured I had better hightail it to our suite before I got in real trouble.

I was going to use another bit of comic relief before I left, but not now. I would only have to envision how things would have gone if I had stood outside the shops crying, and when someone walked up to see what was wrong and if they could help me, tell them that my goldfish died, and even CPR didn't work. Some people don't know how attached a person can get to their goldfish. I was going to tell whoever came up to me that my goldfish and I were movie companions. She sat beside me and we watched *The Little Mermaid* and *Free Willy*. We were watching *Piranha Part Two: The Spawning* when I turned to her and saw her floating to the top of her bowl. The autopsy said she died of a heart attack. I should have known that movie was too much for her. She hid in her cave for three days after we saw *Jaws*. And I would tell them how I had Bubbles cremated, and I have her ashes in a thimble on my mantle.

But then maybe it's good that I never got to tell that story. I can just picture Jennifer and me, and Lou and Thelma Lou in one of the dining rooms and someone comes up to our table telling me again how touched they were about my Bubbles story.

I could picture Jennifer saying, "Bubbles?"

And our visitor says, "That must have been before you two met."

And then Jennifer, with her devious mind, asks, "Was she a dancer whose balloons you popped?"

And our visitor replies, "Oh, no. she was his goldfish, who died, even though he tried to give her CPR. It's her ashes in the thimble on your mantle."

Then Jennifer would look first at me and then our visitor, and wonder which of us is the craziest.

Yes, it's best that I didn't get to share that story with anyone. And I'm sure that somewhere there is someone who would believe it. And someone who might have done that. I used to think most people were sane, and then I discovered the internet.

15

I took another nap and dreamed I was holding the woman of my dreams in my arms. I woke up and found out it was true. And she was kissing me. When I was fully awake, I told her how good she looked and smelled. She didn't tell me how badly I smelled. She told me how good she felt. I didn't tell her that I felt much better at that moment than I did on the archery course. She said she might forget the festivities and go for more spa treatments. I didn't tell her I was going to give up looking for a murderer and shoot more arrows into the air. She didn't ask me how archery went, and I was thankful. I eased off the bed as best I could and headed for the shower. I wanted to clean up and walk around the place before dinner.

+++

Although the first get-together was about to take place, the resort wasn't all that crowded. I wondered if all of this was a joke by Annabelle to get me up here alone. I wanted to find out how busy the place was. The best way to find that out was to go to the check-in place. It was about the time that most people who would be checking in would start to check in. The lobby area had a few people checking in. Maybe this home swap thing was real after all. Maybe Derek and Annabelle weren't going off to stay with his or her mother, and it wasn't his cousin who was coming to stay at their house. Besides, I had seen a couple of people with a lanyard that looks like mine.

I saw a guy with a "Want to Trade" button on his shirt. I figured he was one of them. Maybe he hadn't received his lanyard yet or had forgotten to put it on. I decided to approach him.

"I see your button. Are you one of them?"

"You bet I am. Are you here for the show?"

"Is that what you call it?"

"You're not a collector?"

"A collector of what?"

"Sports cards. I even got a Mickey Mantle rookie card at the last show. The guy didn't know what it was worth. I got it for a song. If I decide to sell it, I can retire for the rest of my life. I guess you're here for something else."

"Home swap."

"Oh, you're in real estate."

"No, it's where people swap their home with someone else for a week or two. Sort of a vacation."

"If I'm going on vacation, I'd rather be at a place like this. If I stayed at somebody else's house, I would have to do my own cooking, wouldn't I?"

"Or go out to eat. But you don't have to pay anything to stay there."

"I'm just here to make some money or get a good deal or two. Got me a Joe Namath card a couple of shows ago. Back when he was doing those pantyhose commercials. Well, I think now he's doing them for Medicare. He's old now, but some women really like him even today. And it's not just guys at these shows. A lot of women come too."

"Well, good luck."

"Good luck to you too. I hope you find yourself a good place to stay."

+++

I decided to spend a few minutes sitting on one of the rockers out on the porch. I went out, chose one, and sat down. I looked around. There was only one other guy on a rocker at that point. I guess the rest were off their rockers. I started to turn back around when I noticed he was thumbing through a copy of *Bad Swap*. While I didn't get a good look, I got enough of a look at the guy who was following Jennifer and me earlier to know that this was a different guy. Still, I got up and approached him. I wanted to see how he might react. I had an advantage on him if he tried to bolt. I was standing and he was sitting.

I opened the conversation.

"I read that book."

"Did you like it?"

"I did. How many copies do you have of it?"

"Excuse me for being so blunt, but that sounds kind of dumb. Why would anyone have more than one copy? And the only reason I have this one is some guy gave it to me. He came up to me and said, 'Would you like to read a good book?' He said, 'No catch. I've already read it, and I'm willing to pass it on. If you'll read it, you can have it.' I saw it was a mystery. I like mysteries. So, I took it."

"Can you describe the guy who gave it to you?"

"I don't know. He was pretty much a normal guy. About your height. A little younger than you. A little thinner than you. His hair was a little lighter than yours."

"Did he tell you his name?"

"No. We only talked for a minute. As soon as he gave me the book, he took off. This was only about ten minutes ago. You said you read the book. Did someone give you your copy?"

"No. I bought it. And the authors are friends of mine. They're here this weekend. Are you part of the home swap group?"

"No. Just here for a little R&R. I come here once a year. Don't know anyone here. Just come here to relax. I'm a pharmaceutical salesman. It can be a stressful job. I manage to take off for a week every three months. I have an employer who realizes that a well-rested employee does a better job than a frazzled one."

"Well, enjoy the book. I did, and I wasn't able to figure out who did it."

"I don't guess you'd make a good detective then."

"I guess not."

"What kind of work do you do?"

"I'm retired."

"You're kind of young to be retired."

"I made my money the old-fashioned way. I inherited it. I did some work for a rich guy, and he was so impressed that a friend and I inherited his money and his house when he died. Well, my friend built a house next door. He and his wife live in it. My wife and I live in the house the dead guy lived in."

"I hope he wasn't murdered in it."

"No. He was murdered somewhere else. I merely solved his murder."

As I said that, I turned and walked away, back inside. I didn't bother to see the look on his face when I told him I solved the author's murder.

+++

I was about to go back to the room when I felt someone put her arms around me. I was pretty sure it wasn't the woman who sat on my rocker. And I didn't think that home swappers were that aggressive to get me to join the group. Well, one of them was. The one who kissed me on the cheek when I turned around.

"Cy, you made it!"

"We've been here for a week, Annabelle."

"I know better than that. A week ago you had never heard of this place."

"Maybe we checked in yesterday."

I figured Jennifer would be upset if I went back to the room and slipped on my swim trunks, so I didn't ask Annabelle to check out the indoor pool with me.

"Derek and I just got in an hour ago. We were wondering if you got here okay."

"We even stopped off in Gettysburg, Hershey, and Pennsylvania Dutch country."

"Any bodies there?"

"There were in Gettysburg, but we didn't dig them up. And we didn't find a murderer there. So, we came up here."

"So you can protect me."

"I'll protect you, Annabelle," Jennifer said, joining the group. "So, this is where you've been, Cy."

"Yes. I've been talking to a guy who collects and sells sports cards."

"Sports card collectors look much different up here than they do at home."

"He's wearing a button that says, "Want to trade.""

"Well, you don't want to trade. Annabelle, where is Derek? He never seems to be around when you are around my husband."

"Here he is now. Derek, look who I found. I was just about to ask Cy and Jennifer if they want to join us for a swim before dinner."

"That sounds great," Derek responded.

"No, they say that swimming before dinner is bad for you," Jennifer replied.

"No, it's after dinner when it is bad for you," Annabelle answered.

"With Cy, it's before dinner," Jennifer volleyed back. "And after dinner is the first session with the murderer and the victims."

With that, we told them we were looking forward to seeing them later, and Jennifer yanked my arm out of its socket pulling me back to our suite.

+++

We stayed in our suite until it was time to call the guy who had probably slipped out for some archery lessons and then we did a repeat of the previous night's dinner. Jennifer said she was sorry that Derek and Annabelle had a different dinner time than we did. I told her that I could arrange to coordinate the same breakfast time and then I ducked. I managed to miss most of the impact of Jennifer's elbow.

+++

We ate another delicious meal of things I don't eat at home and headed back to the room to brush our teeth and give us a chance to check our hair to make sure it was combed properly. Then, we met our other twosome in the hall, and we headed to the room where the murderer might be lurking.

As soon as we walked into that room, I could see it wasn't what I expected. I expected a bunch of people standing around, moving from person to person, getting to know each other. Instead, we walked into the large room and were instructed to take seats, husband and wife together, but not across from anyone we know or have already met. And we weren't to talk to the people at our table, or any other, until we were instructed to do so. That gave me time to look over the room.

I looked at the tables. There were two seats on each side of a table, then a break of a couple of feet before the next table. There appeared to be enough seats to accommodate around one hundred or so people. Maybe a few more than that. We headed over to the wall on one side of the room. Lou and Thelma Lou sat a table up from us, not close enough that we could talk unless we leaned over and talked loudly. The room began to fill up. Two women sat down across from us. I wondered if they were a couple.

They didn't appear to be, but they seemed to be together. More than likely, we would find out soon enough.

When the room seemed to be as full as it was going to get, I spotted Derek and Annabelle halfway across the room. I saw Rhonda Stephens, the bow and arrow expert, and her husband, Nick. Then I noticed a man and woman arose to get us started. Either that or they realized that the great detective Cy Dekker was in their midst, and they figured they might as well confess and get it over with. Their opening line didn't sound like a confession.

"This is the first of our Meet and Greet sessions. You are to get to know the couple or individuals seated on the other side of your table. To help you, there is a question for you to answer to get you started. In a few minutes, a gong will sound. Those of you on the left side of your table," they raised their hand to indicate that Jennifer and I were on the left side of our table, "will then get up and move to the next table. Those on the right side of the table will remain seated and will be joined by another individual or couple. Any questions?"

The attendees seemed to be reasonably smart or were going to hide their ignorance, because no one raised a hand to ask a question. No one saw that I would soon be on the other side of their table and rose to confess either.

+++

In a few seconds, we found out that our tablemates were Nanci Powers and Diana Tellefsen from Tennessee. Both are married, but not to each other. They came up to check out what home swapping is all about. Nanci said she would rather live in Kentucky, and Diana said she would rather retire and live in a library. Diana and I talked about our love for reading. I think she reads more than I do, and she would read more if she had the time. Neither of them needed inspiration from our ice-breaker question, so none of us bothered to look at it. I didn't even ask them if they knew any of the couples I was asking people about. Maybe Lou would ask them if he met them.

+++

When the gong sounded, we got up and moved on. I looked at the couple who didn't have to move. They looked like a couple who would rather spoil their grandkids than someone who would keep someone from having any.

"We're Marvin and Pat Wiley from North Carolina. I like Bugs Bunny and my favorite comic strip is *Baby Blues*."

"Is that what our question is? We didn't need it at our first table."

"It's my favorite cartoon character and favorite comic strip character. My character would be Hammy, unless I would have to put up with him. Then I would get out a gag and handcuffs."

"Well, I'm Cy Dekker and this is my wife, Jennifer. I like Wile E. Coyote, your namesake. He never gets any credit for painting some of the most beautiful tunnels known to mankind. And I love the great philosopher, Snoopy. Although I wouldn't want to sit on top of a doghouse all day and eat dog food. But he's brilliant like I am. And I think someone should always carry a pair of handcuffs with them. One never knows when they might need them."

"And a gag," Jennifer added.

Marvin laughed. I don't know if he was laughing at my witticism or Jennifer's. I wasn't going to ask him.

"And what else are you, Cy, other than modest?"

"You'll have to ask my wife that, but please don't. She lies more than I do."

We spent a few minutes talking to a couple I think I would like to spend more time with, as long as they haven't killed anyone. Normally, people who love their grandchildren don't kill other people unless those people are trying to harm their grandchildren.

16

Half of us continued to play musical chairs. We moved on to a woman seated alone. She didn't look like someone who had murdered her husband, or anyone else's husband or wife. But then a lot of murderers look that way. But most of them don't have pretty white hair like she did. Her hair looked older than she did. She looked like someone who earned her white hair early. I wondered if she had a husband at one time who caused it. Or a neighbor.

We sat down. She introduced herself as Rhonda Richardson from Georgia. She was quite a peach. She told us she used to drive a school bus, so I knew then that she was capable of murder if provoked. Well, at least inflicting pain. She came across as someone who's smart, someone you could have fun with, and someone who might toilet paper the trees in someone's yard, maybe even fork and rice their yard, and then ask God for forgiveness. I asked her if she knew any of the three couples that brought me to this place. She said "no". I couldn't tell if she was lying. That meant she might be a good poker player. She jumped when the gong sounded that it was time for us to move on to the next victim, or murderer. I wondered if that meant she was guilty of more than I thought she was guilty of. I took one last glance at her to see if she was strong enough to toss a man into her trunk, then haul him out of it and place him on someone's couch. Of course, she would have had to have held a woman underwater too. Sometimes that is harder to do than knocking a man out and hauling him from place to place. I tried to remember if Drake Peabody had been knocked out. I knew that his wife had been held underwater until she died. How strong of a person would it have taken to accomplish these two things? Could a woman have done it? Of course, a woman could. I figured Jennifer could have done it if she was determined or mad enough. But then Jennifer has an alibi for the two murders. She was with me. Which means I have an alibi too. It was time to quit thinking of strong women and move on.

+++

We moved on to a couple who had something in common with us. Their marriage hadn't lasted long. Yet. They too were newlyweds. And they too had passed twenty a few years ago. And they too are from Kentucky. I began to wonder if there is anyone left in My Old Kentucky Home.

"We're Raven and Chuck Spalding."

"Raven is an unusual name."

"I don't know many Cys either."

"I'm the only one I know. But there have been others. The only other raven I know hung out with Edgar Allan Poe."

She laughed. She might have been planning my demise at that moment. I refrained from looking under the table to see if she had a certain book ready to put next to me after I succumbed. She spoke before I could find a way to check.

"I'm handicapped. I have to go to work every day when I would rather be home reading a good murder mystery."

I wondered if that meant she let someone else plan her murders for her. She probably lives close to one murder scene. I'd have to keep an eye on her.

"Do you have kids?"

"A few."

I wondered if that meant she had disposed of previous husbands. I looked at Chuck. He didn't seem to be afraid of her. But then, maybe she had sneaked up on the others too. Or maybe there was only one other one, and they parted on friendly terms. I wasn't going to ask. I didn't want to be her next victim. I told her that we were only checking out the home-swapping thing, that we hadn't joined yet. Neither of them volunteered as to whether or not they were a part of it. Maybe he was in on getting rid of a previous husband.

"Are you familiar with Derek and Annabelle Oxley?"

"How should I know them?"

"They write murder mysteries about home swapping. You said you read a lot."

"I said I'd like to stay home and read a lot. I'll have to check out their books. Are they here?"

"They are. What about Howard and Gwen Higginbotham and Drake and Amanda Peabody?"

"Peabody sounds familiar. Do they write too?"

"No. Just part of this group. Until they dropped out."

"They didn't like it?"

"I don't know. I didn't get a chance to ask them."

She smiled when the gong sounded, and we got up to move on to the next table. I wasn't sure if she was planning my murder or not, but she had some idea in that head of hers. I just knew one thing. If there were two sides and she was on one of them, I wouldn't want to be on the other side. And she looked capable of what it would take physically to murder the two dead people. I pitied the person who would cross her, whether she had murdered anyone or not. I was sure she had read a lot of books, maybe even some of them at work. Maybe even one where a woman was drowned and one where there was a body in the trunk of a car.

+++

I sized up the next couple as we approached them.

"Stephanie Beck. Some people call me Steph. This is my husband, Larry. We're from Missouri. We get around."

I wondered if that meant they were wanted by the authorities in one or more states.

We introduced ourselves. Then she spoke again.

"I don't think you noticed, but I saw you at dinner. You look like a private detective who is hired by a wife to find out if her husband is cheating on her. So, tell me what you think about me. Go ahead. Don't hold back."

I wondered if there was more than one murderer in the room. Maybe Steph and Raven were in on it together. Two women can drown a third woman or throw a man in a trunk or yank him out of one easier than one woman can.

"Okay. You look like a person who drinks a lot. Probably wine. More than likely the expensive stuff. I think you got deported from Italy once. You appear to be a person who relates better to dogs than people unless those people are kids or teenagers. And if you have to work, you prefer to do it at some kind of sports event, swimming pool, or at a beach. But preferably not at all. In other words, you're probably more fun to be around than most people, but more likely to be a killer, provided she has a reason. I don't think you would kill someone just to jack up your numbers. Larry is probably afraid of you, but I doubt if the dogs are. I picture you as someone who has more than one dog. I think you're someone I want on my side in a fight. Especially if your pack of dogs are with you. How did I do?"

"I guess I was wrong. You have been following me. How did you know about Italy?"

"Who do you think put the authorities on to you?"

"You were wrong about one thing. I do like some people. But dogs and kids are more fun. Most adults don't know how to have fun."

"I have to agree with you there."

I asked them if they knew any of the couples I was asking people about. They said they didn't know any of them. She seemed honest, but I decided not to ask her if she had killed anyone in the last couple of weeks.

+++

When it came time to move on to the next table, we might have found the only guy who was there by himself, other than the ones I had already met. He looked more like a preacher than a murderer. Of course, somewhere there has to be someone who is both. I have friends who are part of congregations where there are preachers who would like to murder one or two troublemakers sitting there listening to what he is saying each week and disagreeing with it.

"Cy Dekker. Kentucky. This is my wife Jennifer."

"Archie Parrish. I'm from Missouri."

"You don't seem as ornery as that Bunker guy."

He laughed.

"I guess you haven't met anyone who knows me. I like to have as much fun as the next guy, but I don't want to be arrested for it."

"That either means you don't do anything too bad, or you don't get caught doing it."

"Something like that. This is some kind of place, isn't it?"

"Bigger than my place back home. So, who is your favorite cartoon character and your favorite comic strip character?"

"You know, of all of the people who have paraded through here, you are the first one to ask that. The cartoon might be Woody Woodpecker. He laughed a lot. The comic strip might be Pogo. You probably never heard of him."

"Can't say that I have."

"He is famous for saying, 'We have met the enemy and he is us.' He was a possum. He was wise, personable, generous, and lived with other animals in the Okefenokee Swamp."

"Sounds like a good friend to have."

"He was. And children and adults enjoyed reading that comic strip."

I asked him if he knew any of the couples I asked the others about. He claimed he didn't know any of them. The gong sounded before we could talk about anything else. That meant it was time to move on, and Archie could tell others about Pogo. I was sure most of them already knew about Woody Woodpecker. If not, they must have just left the convent or the monastery.

+++

I looked at my watch. We only had time to meet two more couples, and nobody stood out so far as a likely suspect. Well, a couple of the women did. Still, I wondered if I was wasting my time by coming here.

I looked at the next couple. She looked harmless, but I wasn't sure about him. He looked like he had friends in high places. Bad places.

"Sonny Lipps. This is my wife, Mary. We're from Kentucky, but we live in Florida now."

As soon as he said Sonny I immediately thought of *The Godfather*. When he said they left Kentucky, I figured there must have been a reason. Either the police or a crime family must have been after them. Him, not them. She looked like someone who loved hugging grandchildren. She might not know what he does or did for a living.

Jennifer saw that my mind was elsewhere, so she introduced us, and told them that we were also from Kentucky, but that we hadn't left. I couldn't believe how many people were here from Kentucky. Only none of the others had left. They still lived in paradise.

Sonny didn't look like the kind of guy you would ask who his favorite cartoon character is. Mary looked like the kind of person you might ask for some recipes, or how many cats she has. She just had the look of a cat person.

I got up my courage and asked them if they knew any of the people most of the other people didn't know. He claimed not to know any of them, either before or after they died. Of course, only one of the couples died. Unless something happened to the Higginbothams since I talked to Howard. If he was somewhere in the same room I was in, I hadn't met him yet.

+++

I couldn't believe it when our last couple of the night told us their names and where they lived. Vicki and John Versetti. Also from Florida. I wondered how many people in this home swap thing were part of the Family. The Lipps had to leave Kentucky. The Versettis had to leave Illinois. A pattern was developing here. They claimed they had been all the way to Key West, but they had never heard of the Peabodys, let alone been to their house on Islamorada. But they did say they met Derek and Annabelle and Vicki was looking forward to reading their books since she was an avid reader. I wondered if there was another reason too. I didn't push it. I watch myself around Italians.

They told us about their house. Two levels. Lots of windows. A pool. Not far from the ocean. Three thousand square feet. I wouldn't mind staying there as long as they were away and none of their relatives came to visit while we were there. Or any male members of the Family visited either.

She said she was a pharmacy tech. I thought about how the Peabodys were killed. I wondered if a pharmacy tech had an advantage over someone else. Maybe an

Italian pharmacy tech might. I also remembered I had met a pharmaceutical representative earlier. Could either of them be responsible for the murders? But then, anyone can hold someone under the water. Definitely, someone who is a part of the Family would know how to do that.

John said he spends his time by the pool and on the golf course. Amanda Peabody spent her final minutes in the pool. I wondered if John spent any time in the same pool. Maybe I was tired. Maybe he was no more guilty than Jennifer was.

The final gong sounded. I did not know for whom the bell tolls. Maybe it tolls for me.

+++

We waited until the others had walked out. Then the four of us walked back to our suite. We had sat across from the same couples except for one. Lou was ready to arrest Sonny Lipps and John Versetti. I told him we'd better wait until we found out if they had alibis for the times of the murders. They might have been in Florida while the Floridians were getting murdered elsewhere.

+++

I thought about the two things that didn't turn out the way I thought they would as I thought of them the night before. There weren't two get-togethers, but one, and we didn't have to stand around and meet people. It was more structured.

The next day was going to be a long one, so all of us decided to turn in early. I made it up my circular staircase without falling. I let Jennifer go first. I liked looking at her climbing above me. She climbed well.

17

We got up early the next morning and practiced our cleanliness and godliness routine. I spent my time with God out on the balcony. I thought it was the perfect place for reading my Bible, devotional books, and praying. Evidently, I didn't pray enough for God to reveal the killer's identity, or even if he or she was spending the weekend with me, in a manner of speaking.

Jennifer didn't need to do anything to look great, but she did those things that women do to get ready. Then we called the other couple, one of whom claimed to have been ready for hours. When I saw him, I told him he should have spent more time working on his face. Her face didn't need it. His body still needed a lot of work. Lou told me I must have been looking in the mirror.

+++

Our morning would be spent eating a buffet breakfast and going for a carriage ride. I wasn't sure if we would have time for anything else. It was 8:15 when we arrived at the dining room. We would be a part of a lunch group. It wouldn't begin until 12:30.

I asked Lou how he felt about breakfast al fresco. The girls had already agreed to try it. Lou told me he had never tried it and asked me how it tasted. I told him that most people like it if the weather is nice, but you have to eat it outside.

I looked over the possibilities.

"Cy, how do you like your bagels?"

"On someone else's plate."

"But they come with some great accompaniments. You have your choice of butter, cream cheese, smoked salmon, sliced tomatoes, red onion, lemon, and capers."

"I'm already involved in a caper. One is enough for me."

I skipped the granola and hot cereal too, but I picked up some apple cinnamon bread. Then I got to the stuff I wanted. Scrambled eggs, breakfast potatoes, Belgian waffles with whipped cream, caramel, bananas, Nutella, and local maple syrup. Then I topped it off with bacon and sausage. The necessary food groups. I think that Lou followed suit, but the girls ate more daintily.

We took our time eating, then looked out at the water. It was a wonderful place to enjoy breakfast. I looked up when I heard my name called. It was Marvin Wiley, one of the guys we met last night. He waved. I waved back. I hoped he didn't see the napkin in my shirt. I hate it when I eat syrup and my shirt looks like a Rorschach test of a lighter color.

It wasn't even 9:00 yet, but I saw two people out in a canoe. The sun was beginning to rise above the trees, but it was still low enough that it wasn't beating down on the water. I liked the different possibilities we had for dining. I was sure that the place where I was eating wasn't a choice for breakfast in February. I doubted if the carriage ride or the tomahawk toss was either. I was sure they had other choices for people to spend their time during the cold weather months. Like building an igloo. If we come back, I might sign up for learning how to build a fire. In a fireplace. For some reason, I wondered if there were any moose nearby. I wondered if all of them were in Canada or out west. I had one at my house once. Bullwinkle. I never thought of him as one of the more gifted moose. Or is it mooses or meese? I think moose are like deer. One or more it's always the same.

+++

The Wileys were the only people we had already met who chose to eat breakfast where and when we were eating. I wondered if that meant they were stalking us. They didn't seem the type. They seemed more like the spring-on-you-out-of-the-dark kind of people. No. Really, I didn't think they looked as murderous as many of the others. That must mean that one of them did it. Probably Marvin. He smiled a lot.

There were a couple of women with lanyards that matched ours who were eating there, but we hadn't met them yet. They probably met each other last night.

+++

We made the trek back inside and back to our suites to brush our teeth. We left in time to make sure that we got to the carriage on time. We wanted to ride forward instead of backward, and we didn't want it to turn into a pumpkin. And I've always preferred horses to rats. Maybe it's a Kentucky thing. You won't find rat races in Kentucky. Or if so, they don't advertise it. I think you find the rat race more in larger cities.

+++

I remembered that my main objective of being where I was wasn't to have fun. I grabbed my cell phone and punched in a number.

"This is Sam I Am. Aren't you supposed to be on vacation?"

"No. I'm supposed to be at a resort catching a murderer. That's the reason I'm calling you."

"You want me to come and join you?"

"No. I want you to check up on some people who have joined me."

"All of them?"

"No. Only thirty or so. But only ten for the time being."

"Cy, I already have plans for the weekend. Not as fancy as your plans. But today is the only day I can give you until Monday. What do you want me to do for you?"

"All I want is to give you a few names. You can check on them and still make it to the roller derby. You tell me if they could have murdered the dead couple whose names we now know. In case you don't know their names, they were Drake and Amanda Peabody from Islamorada, Florida. She was found in Hilldale. He was found in North Carolina. Are you ready to write?"

"I'm writing and recording. Shoot."

"Nanci Powers and Diana Tellefsen from Tennessee. They are both married, but their husbands stayed at home. Check on their whereabouts at the time of the murders. See if they could have done it. The same is true for the others.

"Rhonda and Nick Stephens, and Raven and Chuck Spalding from Kentucky, but not the same place. Marvin and Pat Wiley from North Carolina. Rhonda Richardson from Georgia. Larry and Stephanie Beck from Missouri. Archie Parrish from Missouri. And Sonny and Mary Lipps, and Vicki and John Versetti from Florida."

"You don't know what towns they live in."

Some of them I did. I told him those towns. The others should be easy for someone of Sam's expertise to find.

"I don't need to know anything else about them except whether or not they had alibis for the times of the murders."

"You're all heart, Cy."

"That's what you keep telling me."

"I'll see what I can find out before I leave town. Otherwise, it will be Monday or later before I know anything."

"I hope your amnesia clears up before then."

"You know what I mean."

"What is your position in this roller derby anyway?"

"I'm the jammer."

"Blackberry or strawberry?"

I thanked Sam, told him to have a good weekend, and hung up. I knew I wasn't going to know about most of these people until after they returned to the homes they wanted to leave again soon. I hoped that none of them were going to leave again to commit another murder.

+++

We were the first to arrive for our carriage ride. The driver allowed us to step up and into the carriage. I checked him out without frisking him. As far as I could tell, he hadn't murdered anyone. At least there wasn't a copy of *Bad Swap* on the seat beside him. And if he planned to kill us, I would think he would have taken off before anyone else showed up. Unless he planned to shoot all of us. And I doubted if he had hit the regular driver over the head just so he could drive us to some remote spot and rob us. I doubted if he knew that Lou and I were carrying. The girls were too, but their guns don't make as big of a hole when it hits you.

We were soon joined by another couple with lanyards that matched ours.

"Hi, I'm Donna Thompson. This is my husband Carl. We're from a small town in Ohio. We scare people. Well, I do."

"How do you do that?"

"Well, I have over two hundred horror movies at home. Plus, some of the characters in those movies hang around my house."

"You don't have many friends, do you?"

"My dogs."

She showed me pictures. People love to show pictures of their animals and their grandkids. I made a note to take pictures of Blue and Quiggley when I got home. If I could keep them still long enough.

"I didn't realize that Spuds Mackenzie belongs to you."

She laughed.

"Saffron's coloring is a little different. And Saffron eats invisible treats."

"So does Lou," I said, pointing at my friend.

"Do you have horror masks or costumes?"

"Of course."

"Do you wear them out in public?"

"Only to the bank."

"When is the last time you killed someone?"

"It's been a few weeks now."

We were getting along well when we were joined by someone who seemed more normal. Which would have been anyone other than except Raven, Steph, Sonny, and John.

The driver helped her into the carriage. She too had on one of our lanyards.

"I'm Mary Sheridan. I'm from Georgia."

"By the way you talked, I thought you were from New York City."

She laughed.

She was a classy-looking lady. I couldn't see her killing a fly, let alone a human. This woman wouldn't watch horror movies. But she would love on her kids and grandchildren. She looked like a woman who loves music, and all kinds of music. Everything from classical, to country, to opera.

Before we could talk much, our final seat was taken. Another woman. This one by Linda Williams, also from Ohio. I looked at her and saw a woman with fond memories of the past, hope for the future, and someone who enjoyed a good laugh. In other words, she wasn't my top suspect.

We were having such a good time that it came as a surprise when the carriage took off. But the driver took off slow enough that I didn't fall out. I wish he would have let me know he was getting ready to move. It would have given me a chance to push Lou out. I tried to look around at our surroundings, while at the same time talking to and listening to those we were sharing our carriage with. The subject of murder never came up.

We men were outnumbered five to three, so we let the women do most of the talking. Jennifer, and even Thelma Lou, told the others about how much they enjoyed their spa treatment. Everyone talked about where they were staying, and what their home and their town were like. I just sat back and took it all in. Lou did too.

No one was so loud that I couldn't enjoy the clip-clop of the horses' hooves. The carriage was drawn by two horses, and as it turned out, everyone was facing forward, so it made it a little harder to have a conversation. But we managed. People have fun doing that. The ones in front of us turned around to talk and to listen. I guess I was having fun. But I was there to catch a killer. I hadn't done that yet. And I wasn't sure if there was a killer to catch here. I would soon know the answer to that.

18

Lunch was to be outdoors with the swappers if the weather was good, and indoors if it wasn't. We had been blessed with good weather the whole time, and nothing changed, so we got to eat down by the lake and, I listened for a splash in case someone decided to use water for a third murder.

This time we were assigned seats, so we would meet different people than we met before. At least these were seats we were to start in. We would be moving from table to table, just like we did last night, only with food this time. We all looked around for our placards. Jennifer found ours and called for me. Someone was already sitting in the seats across from us. This time we were told to talk about the house and area where we live. We were told to head to the salad table, put two or three items on a plate, and sit down. I got a small portion of tuna salad and fruit salad, and a couple of watermelon wedges. I was living dangerously. Jennifer chose only the heirloom tomato and cucumber salad. We set our plates on the table, and someone came and took our drink order. I introduced Jennifer and myself as we were sitting down. It didn't take me long to find out the guy was a character.

"We're Jim and Debra Burns from North Carolina. We live in the woods, sit on our front porch with our guns loaded, shoot at anything that moves, and if nothing comes to us, we send the dog out to fetch it.

"We go to the state fair, Dairy Queen on Saturday, and the Baptist Church every Sunday. When we get the itch to do something different, we swap homes with someone else, tell them the dog won't bite, and where we keep his food."

When he paused, I started talking.

"We live in the woods too. We sit on the front porch part of the time. We don't have our guns with us, because nothing ever comes by except the next-door neighbor and my wife won't let me shoot him, because he married her cousin. We have a deck and a hot tub in the back. Sometimes my wife makes me go for a walk in the woods, but there is nothing to shoot there, either. We have a dog, but he won't fetch anything. And we have a duck too. He flew in one day and doesn't leave, even in the winter."

We all laughed and both women knew that Baptist women everywhere were praying for both of the wives because they have to live with us. He finally admitted that he is jealous because he doesn't have a duck. His wife told him that if one flew in, he would shoot it, so he shut up. The gong sounded about that time, and we moved on to the next table. On the way to that table, as the breeze messed up my hair, I whispered to Jennifer.

"But they live in North Carolina. Maybe they dropped one of the bodies off on the way home."

"It's always the quiet one, Cy. Do you think she did it?"

"You might have something there."

+++

We dumped our plates in the trash, and headed for the next table. I was really living dangerously this time. It was time for the main course. A couple of guys were there grilling, and they seemed to have whatever we wanted. Our choices were so extensive that there was a board there with all of the choices on it. I looked it over and opted for a barbecue sandwich with baked beans and macaroni and cheese. I could tell it had never been in a box. I chose an ear of grilled corn on the cob with melted butter and queso fresco. Jennifer wasn't going to be as messy. She selected a smoked turkey breast, roasted potatoes, and summer vegetables. It was time to meet our next set of suspects. As soon as we set our plates down, someone was there to refill our drinks.

The next couple spoke first.

"We're Tom and Carol Anderson from Indiana."

"Indiana? Do you know what they call a speed bump in Indiana? A scenic overlook."

I couldn't tell if they liked my joke or not.

We introduced ourselves before I took a bite. Tom and Carol didn't have to move, so they were already into their lunch. It took them a minute to answer my comment.

"Now, Cy, there are some hills in Indiana."

"Not in the parts where I've been. But go ahead. I don't want to interrupt."

"Well, our house is not as large as some of the ones in the home exchange. It's only 2,775 square feet. We have a large front porch with rockers and a glider out front, with a wooded area to look out upon. And wide-open spaces and a deck out back, with a swimming pool. Inside, we have an eighty-five-inch TV, over two thousand movies, over two hundred TV series, and all the sports channels. We also have a library with a couple of thousand books, mainly mystery, romance, and fantasy, since that is what people are mainly interested in these days. All of those things are the drawing cards for people wanting to swap homes with us, not the fact that we have a large, fancy home. And we don't travel a lot."

I told them we were not yet home swappers but were meeting people in the group. I asked them about the three couples, and they said they didn't know any of them. I couldn't gauge whether they were telling the truth or not.

+++

There were desserts, but we decided to wait for two or three more introductions before trying them.

We moved on to Judy and Bob Williams from Georgia. They have some mileage on them, but they don't seem to be slowing down. They live out in the woods too, but they don't shoot people. At least they didn't claim to shoot anyone who came calling. They have a big house, but that is because people are always welcome there, and the more people, the merrier. Family is important to them unless Georgia is playing a football game. But then I think they brought their kids up to know that they either need to be at the game or watching it wherever they are. They don't cotton to those people from Tuscaloosa, but they might pray for them. They seem to like both old people and young people and did their best to populate the world and teach their kids to do the same. If it had been that Roll Tide couple who had been murdered, I might suspect the Williamses, but since it wasn't, I don't think they're the ones we're looking for.

+++

Next, we met Jane and Phil Bellomy from California. Jennifer and Jane did most of the talking here. Jennifer told her where we live. Jane told Jennifer she loved animals. Jennifer told her that we have a dog and a duck. Jane said, "Only one of each?" She pointed at me and said, "He only has one wife too." Jane said, "I only have one husband, but I like to love on lots of animals. Living in the woods can enable you to have lots of animals." Jennifer let her know that only one duck flew in and stayed and only one dog adopted me but is more spoiled by her. Anyway, they have a nice place in the wilderness and are adventuresome, even to the point of going whitewater rafting and tromping through the woods. That is if there are no dogs, cats, small horses, or other animals to be loved on. I'm sure she didn't kill any animals. I'm not sure about people. She said their house is about what you would expect from someone like her. I'm not sure what that means.

+++

The next one we met was a single woman, Terry Reed. She's originally from Lexington, Kentucky but lives in Jefferson County, in a house overlooking the Ohio River. She loves to go sit high up on the riverbank and look down upon the river at the traffic moving up and down the river. She wonders where each one is going and why, or if they are just out for the day. She often wonders if she would like to get on one of those riverboats and take it down to New Orleans, stopping at each port of call. They are not nearly as large as those cruise ships, but much more expensive to travel on. She said her house is nothing special, but some people are looking for nothing special or to get away from it all. She is not yet one of them and is just here checking it out. She heard about it from a friend. She's interested in finding out all she can about home swapping tomorrow. She never heard of any of the people I mentioned, not even our former neighbors, the authors.

+++

Let's see. The next couple we met was Richard and Susan Clark from Tennessee. They appeared to be a couple who enjoys a simple life. Susan said they live in a small house in the woods. She likes to take walks in a meadow nearby with her dog whom she named Snoopy. She picks flowers there and brings them home and puts them in a vase. She likes reading and working word puzzles. They came here to find out if anyone would be interested in swapping homes for a week or two and staying in a small cottage in the woods. She assured me that she is not a witch and had done no harm to any small children. Surely, she is the killer we are seeking.

+++

I was ready for dessert, so we visited the large dessert table before we met our next couple. There weren't as many dessert choices as there were grilled items, but there were enough. I chose a piece of coconut pie and an almond raspberry tart. Jennifer stopped with one dessert. A piece of pecan pie.

We sat down across from Craig and Merry Sautter, from way out in Oregon. He was drooling when he saw my dessert, so I showed him my fork. He backed off. I figure he had already put away two or three desserts of some sort and talked his wife into putting a couple more in her purse. We found out that they love to travel, so coming here was no big deal for them. And by the way, her name is Merry as in Christmas. With a name like Merry, she must be the killer.

"We live in a unique house in the woods. Seems like a lot of these people live in the woods. It has windows all around, with drapes for privacy, and shutters to keep us warm in the winter. We can see the forest on one side and a lake on another. We have a porch on the first floor and a deck on the second, where our bedrooms are. We don't have a pool, but we do have a hot tub. We travel some. We went to Alaska and Yellowstone. There are bears in them thar woods. We are new at this and have only been to California for a home exchange."

+++

I didn't go back to the dessert table. I might have tried that if I were alone, but I wasn't, so I hurried the short distance to the next table to meet a woman who sat there alone. Jennifer sat down and I followed suit. We introduced ourselves.

"I'm Pamela Sober. I'm from Louisiana."

"Who are you when you are drunk?"

"No one knows who they are when they are drunk. That's the reason if they are drunk, they should stay home and lock themselves in a room until they are sober again." I agreed with that, but I wanted to see if I could get a rise out of her, so I asked the following question.

"Are people civilized in Louisiana?"

"Only a few. We pray for them. In answer to the question we are supposed to answer, I live in a castle, complete with a moat with no gators. It has a drawbridge, turrets, the works. People are always showing up, wanting to see the inside."

Jennifer said, "Really?"

"No. I live in a house like everyone else. When I want to have fun, I go up to the attic and rummage through some boxes. More times than not, I end up with a photograph album, turn the pages, and reminisce. I can spend hours doing that. Then I remember where I am, and scamper back downstairs to the real world."

I asked her if she had heard of any of the couples I mentioned.

"I met Derek and Annabelle last night. It made my weekend. I've been reading their books for a while. That's where I first heard about home swapping. Then through their website, I heard about this weekend. It gave me a chance to meet them and find out more about what this is all about. I almost had to mortgage my home to come, but here I am."

I was looking at another person I didn't think was the killer I was seeking. Was that person here or off somewhere else killing someone else?

+++

We were informed that we had time to get to know one other person or couple. Our one person turned out to be Carolyn Summerlin, another Georgia person.

"You look happy," I said.

"I am," she replied. "After all, I do live in Georgia."

"What's great about Georgia?"

"It's the only state that has Jimmy Carter. He keeps blessing people, even at his age. Not as much as God does, but more than most humans. And I have my Atlanta sports teams, and my church. So, I'm pretty happy."

"I am too, and I don't have any of that except God and my church. But my wife more than makes up for Jimmy Carter, and she's a lot better looking. And she probably cooks better than he does."

"Well, you do look like you've eaten regular."

I laughed. Then shut up, and let Jennifer get her two cents worth in. Before I knew it, our time was up.

19

On our way up the steps, I spotted an older woman, probably around eighty, leaning on a cane. She saw me looking at her, so she spoke to me.

"How do I get one of them necklaces like all of you got?"

"We're part of a group."

"Some kind of religion?"

"No. A home swap group."

"You mean you trade your house for someone else's even steven?"

"In a way. But only for a week or two. Like for a vacation."

"You mean I have to let somebody else stay at my house?"

"Yeah. And you get to stay at theirs. And both of you have to agree that you want to stay in each other's house."

"I don't think I'd like that. I like to stay at a bed-and-breakfast."

"Then why are you here? This isn't a bed-and-breakfast."

"My daughter and son-in-law paid for it."

"What's your name and where are you from?"

"You're not trying to make me one of your bunch, are you? I don't want one of them necklaces that much."

"No. just trading names. I'm Cy. I'm from Kentucky."

"Well, then, I'm Maggie. I'm from Ohio. Pleased to meet you, Cy. I'd best be going."

She moved on, slowly, but she still looked back now and then, curious about all of the people wearing lanyards like mine. She seemed to be alone.

+++

I noticed that Lou was exercising his right arm. One guy mistook him for a Florida State fan. Lou didn't understand what the guy meant. When the guy explained, Lou told him he was warming up for the tomahawk toss. I knew he didn't want to embarrass himself again, like he did when he tried to shoot a bow and arrow. Maybe when we get home, I can have Joey teach him how to do it.

Lou and I cried when we parted ways from the girls. I wanted them to think we were going to miss them. It wasn't that I expected them to spend too much money shopping. It is that I am afraid that someone knows who we are and will get a video of Lou and me throwing a tomahawk and send it back to a certain two guys back in Hilldale.

Lou and I made it to the place of doom. We received our instructions and were thankful there wasn't a big crowd. And there was no one from Home Swappers Anonymous there. So, we won't get laughed at when we gather with the others tonight.

Lou motioned for me to go first this time. We were throwing at a figure. I took too careful of an aim and then threw. I hit the board and Lou laughed. My guy would be a soprano forever. I threw my second tomahawk. He would also have a headache for life.

I stepped aside and motioned for Lou to beat my throws. Lou rocked back and forth, aimed, and threw. They needed a wider board. In truth, Lou only missed the board by six inches, but when we get home the length of his miss will grow to two feet.

"It slipped," my friend said.

He reached down and rubbed some dirt on his hands. This time, as he was warming up, he almost lost some toes.

"Try grease," I said.

He picked it up and heaved it at the figure without rocking or aiming. It hit the guy right in the heart. He turned to me and bowed. I applauded. A young lady, who had not seen his mishaps and was not a part of our group, stepped up to feel his muscles. I took their picture together. I planned to show it to Thelma Lou later.

We stayed there awhile and watched some others, most of whom were more graceful than we were.

+++

We arrived back at our suite just in time to see someone trying doorknobs. When he saw me, he took off. He was too young and too fast for me to catch him, but I reported him to security. I did see him head out the front door. I doubted if he was anyone staying there. I knew it wasn't anyone I had seen. He was quite young.

+++

On the way back to the room, we spotted a couple of shoppers who looked like they could be picked up. I mentioned that to Lou, and he headed for one of them. I shoved him aside, and he moved on to the other one.

"I see you've been spending some of my hard-earned money."

"Not enough of it, but we'll be here awhile longer."

We dropped off Jennifer's purchases in the room and went for a stroll. We walked enough that I needed a nap when I got back to the suite. I was tired enough that she had to push me up the staircase. I got to the bedroom and saw something on the bed, something that wasn't there when I left it this morning. There were two Hershey Almond candy bars and two Maple Bun candy bars.

"Where did these come from?"

"This is a high-class place. Maybe they leave something on your pillow better than mints."

"Maybe it was a sneaky wife."

"I've been out shopping. It couldn't have been me. Maybe it was another sneaky wife."

I noticed that the Hershey Almond bars looked like they had been opened. I decided to investigate. I opened one of them and started laughing. Each candy bar had been broken to where each piece contained one almond, just the way I like it.

"And how did someone else's wife know how I like to eat these?"

"The Easter Bunny knows lots of things."

"Did Lou get candy too?"

"He did."

"But Lou wasn't good this year."

"That's the reason his candy was late."

"Why was my candy late?"

Jennifer just looked at me with a smile on her face.

"But my candy shouldn't be late because Lou was bad."

I put my arms around her and gave her a big and lasting "thank you" kiss. Then I plopped one piece of a Hershey Almond bar into my mouth, took my shoes off, and lay down on the bed.

"Cy, the Easter Bunny took all of Lou's M&Ms out of the bags and did a color-coded design on the bed."

As she said that she took her phone and showed me a picture. I wondered if Lou ran his mouth all over the bed gobbling up M&Ms, or if he put some of them back in the bags for later. I quit thinking about that when I yawned. I was tired. I think I went to sleep before all the chocolate melted in my mouth, but I did chew and swallowed the nut first.

After I woke up, I hollered for Jennifer and tried to pull her into the shower with me, but she was having none of that. I was going to turn the water to cold and step out.

+++

I called Sam. He accused me of rushing him. He had mixed emotions when I told him I wasn't rushing him. I merely had more people for him to check on. I gave him the names of the people we had met since Sam and I had last chatted. He told me that it would be better if I stayed in my suite. Then he told me that he had eliminated four of the people I had given him so far. It turned out to be four people I was sure had not murdered anyone.

20

Dinner was on our own in the Main Dining Room, which was surprising to me, and it was a little earlier than last night because the festivities were starting a little earlier. That would give us a chance to meet more people. On the way down the hall, an attractive woman, around forty, turned the corner on the wrong side and bumped into me.

"Oh, sorry, Cy. I wasn't watching where I was going." And like that she was off in a flash.

"Who was that?" my jealous wife asked.

"I honestly don't know. I've never seen her before. And her voice didn't sound familiar"

"Well, she certainly knows who you are."

I turned to Lou, but he was no help. I was so surprised that I didn't notice if she had a lanyard on or not. I asked the others. Thelma Lou said she didn't think she had one on, but she couldn't be sure. I tried to forget about it and concentrated on what would be for dinner. I was pretty sure it wasn't going to be something Kinsey Millhone was used to eating. I didn't think most people would be dressed like she likes to dress either. Or like I like to dress either. We ace detectives have to make changes sometimes.

+++

We ate another enjoyable dinner and headed for the large room where we would play "find the murderer." Some people had found out who Derek and Annabelle were, and they were signing books. I didn't see a book table, so I figured each of these people had brought the books that were being signed. Should I go and look at each book, see if it was personalized to someone, and see if that book ends up next to a dead body before we leave? Probably not. Then I would have to let everyone know that I'm the world's best detective since Inspector Clouseau. Or is it Lt. Columbo?

We got there and found out that this time we could mill around and meet whomever we wanted. Several people had beaten us to the room. I looked around for the attractive redhead who attacked me on the way to dinner. Redheads, like blondes, stick out in a crowd. I didn't see her anywhere. I wondered if she might be a pickpocket working the resort, so I checked my pockets. Nothing was missing.

I looked at this one woman checking me out. I could tell she was a hoot and a holler. Like maybe she hadn't been out of jail long. I looked down to see if she was wearing an ankle bracelet. She probably thought I was checking out her figure. She smiled at me. The guy with her didn't notice. Maybe he was her parole officer. She had "murderer" written all over her face. I was sure everyone in the Church of God was praying for her. I walked up to them, Jennifer by my side.

"Hi, I'm Cy Dekker."

"I'm Roxine Stone. This is my husband Rick. We're from Tennessee."

"I guess you can't help that. I'm from Kentucky."

"Had to go out and buy shoes before you came?" she asked.

"Only one. My pappy left one when he ran away. Actually, I have a friend who's an amputee. He happened to lose the leg of the one where I needed a shoe. He sold it to me for a dollar."

She laughed.

"Roxine, I think you've met your match," were the first words out of Rick's mouth.

It was then that I found out he could talk too, but I expect he didn't get much of a chance to at home.

"So, are you here to swap?" I asked.

"You got a wife you're willing to trade?" Rick asked. "She's mighty pretty."

I wasn't sure if the woman he was calling pretty was his wife or mine. Maybe he and Roxine were equally yoked. I remembered they were from Tennessee. They were probably cousins.

"I'd better keep her. I think she might shoot better than you do, even though you are from Tennessee. So, you are a part of this group?" I asked, trying to get serious again.

"I guess. We're kinda new at this. Some people tell me when they come to our place it's the first time they've ever used an outhouse. I tell them that not everybody in our neck of the woods has a two-holer. That's for sisters and in case you have female company, since women like to go in pairs. I know because I'm a woman, you see. I'm an expert in what women do."

I was glad Roxine added that last part. And I was pretty sure that Roxine and Jennifer didn't do the same things. Well, not all of the same things.

"We live in the woods too, but our bathroom is inside the house. Do you know any of these people?" I asked.

"We were hoping to meet some people whose houses we have stayed in."

"So, you didn't leave any of the houses in too bad of shape?"

"Nope. We even washed out the bathtub we slept in before we left."

"Do you know Derek and Annabelle Oxley, Howard and Gwen Higginbotham, or Drake and Amanda Peabody?"

"Friends of yours?"

"The Oxleys are. I met one of the others, and talked to one of the others on the phone."

"Well, none of those names seem familiar. We haven't stayed at any of their places."

I noticed that they didn't cringe when I mentioned any of the names.

"Well, I'll let you meet some people whose houses you have stayed in. Good to meet you."

"You too."

+++

I noticed another couple not talking to anyone, so I approached them. On my way, I noticed that Lou and Thelma Lou were talking to someone. This time I was the one who almost bumped into someone. This time the woman spoke first.

"Enjoying yourself?"

"We are. Are you on the staff here?"

"No. Just one of the minglers. I'm Cy from Kentucky. This is my wife Jennifer."

Jennifer stepped from behind me, as the room was getting more crowded.

"You're a long way from home. I'm Anne and this is my husband Mark. We're the Perkins. We're from almost next door. New Hampshire. The White Mountains."

"I bet it's pretty there."

"It is. I understand Kentucky is pretty too. Green grass and horses."

"You understand correctly. Do you belong to this group?"

She laughed.

"If you can belong to a group where you don't know anyone. Do you and your wife swap homes?"

"Not yet. We have a neighbor who invited us. They invited us to join them this weekend. And our next-door neighbor and his wife came too. We came to find out all we can about the group. See what people like and don't like. How about you? What do you like and don't you like?"

"We can't think of anything we don't like yet. We've been doing this for a while, enjoyed every place we have been."

"Do you know Derek and Annabelle Oxley?"

"Only by name. We read their books. Are they here? We'd love to meet them."

"They are, but they are talking to someone right now. Have you read their book *Bad Swap* yet?"

"Yes. It was a good one."

"What about Howard and Gwen Higginbotham?"

"No. Don't know them. Do they write too?"

"No, but they've swapped homes with the Oxleys. What about Drake and Amanda Peabody?"

"It's hard to answer that one."

"Why?"

"Well, we've stayed in their house in the Keys, and they've stayed in ours, but we've never met them. Love their house though. It worked out great for both of us. We traded in the winter. See we have a three-level A-frame in the mountains. They have a three-level house on the water. They were interested in skiing in the winter. We were interested in going someplace warmer. That's the good thing about this group. Everyone seems to have what someone else wants."

"Do you know anyone else who has stayed at the Peabody's house or someone who knows them?"

"No. Can't say we do. Hopefully, before the weekend is over, we'll get to meet enough people and make some friends and find out about other places we can go. I guess the bad thing about this place is that when you get where you're going, you're alone there."

"The Peabody's house intrigues me. Can you tell me anything about the place or anything you might have learned about them by staying there?"

"Why are you so nosy about them?"

"Just curious. By the way, I see Derek and Annabelle just left the couple they were talking to and are headed this way. Do you want me to introduce you?"

"Sure."

When I mentioned Derek and Annabelle again, their skeptical faces turned to smiles.

+++

After I made introductions and told Derek and Annabelle that the other couple was fans of theirs, I looked around for my next target. Well, first I made notes, so I wouldn't forget whom I had talked to.

I caught another couple not talking to anyone. They looked to be in their late thirties or early forties. They smiled as I approached.

"Here alone?"

"No. My wife is trying to make her way through the crowd. Here she is. I'm Cy Dekker. The late arrival is my wife Jennifer. We're from Kentucky."

"Well, we are Karl and Kristin Olson. We're from Minnesota."

"Oh, God's frozen people."

They laughed.

"Sometimes. We do cross-country skiing, snowmobiling, ice fishing, a lot of things they don't do in Florida."

"How big is your igloo?"

They laughed again.

"Two floors. And we have a pet grizzly."

I knew they were kidding me then.

"How long have you been doing this?"

"Almost since we got married. Ten years. We've done bed-and-breakfast places too, but we like this better. We are doing more of this and fewer bed-and-breakfast places. We told one woman we weren't coming back because we were going to do home swaps exclusively. I think she got mad."

"Really?"

"Really. A place not too far from here. Not in New York though."

"And what is your favorite place you have been?"

"Alaska. It kept us from being homesick."

I wasn't sure if they were kidding me or not.

They were smiling the whole time.

"Do you ever go south, like to Florida, on your home swaps?"

"We swapped homes once with a couple who lives near Disney World. We went there. Universal too. We loved it, except for the long lines. We've stayed in eleven states so far, counting bed and breakfasts."

"Do you have a favorite state?"

"Our favorite state is Colorado. Our favorite place is Jackson Hole, Wyoming. But we have enjoyed lots of places. Niagara Falls, Williamsburg, a few places in California, western Washington state."

"Let me ask you if you know any of these couples who do home swaps. Derek and Annabelle Oxley, Howard and Gwen Higginbotham, or Drake and Amanda Peabody."

"I don't think so. I know we haven't stayed in any of their homes. Where do they live?"

"Kentucky, North Carolina, and the Florida Keys."

"Where did you say you're from, Cy?"

"Kentucky."

"Do you know all of those couples?"

"I know the couple in Kentucky. I own a house next door to theirs. I've seen the woman from the Florida Keys. I've talked to the man in North Carolina, but I've never seen him. I have no idea if he is here or not. I don't know what he looks like."

"That's the funniest thing about this group. We talked to a couple on our way to dinner. Five minutes into our conversation we realized that we had stayed in each other's home."

Again, they both laughed. They appeared to be a fun-loving couple and not capable of murdering anyone. I told them it was nice talking to them and left to meet someone else.

21

Time was flying by, and I had only talked to three people or couples at this session. There was no way that we were going to be able to talk to everyone unless we stayed until midnight. And everyone else stayed that late. And we probably wouldn't even be able to talk to everyone even then. Maybe there was something to be said for having the gong to move us along. I looked for my next prey. As I did, I wondered if the murderer was in the room looking for his or her next prey.

I noticed one couple who looked like they were having too good of a time. Well, the wife was. I wondered if she was planning her next murder or was just a party animal. Other than the guys who seemed to be part of the Mafia, most of the likely murder suspects seemed to be women. Could it be that the murderer is a woman?

I went up and introduced myself to that couple.

"I'm Kimberly Crenshaw and this is my husband, David. We're from Montana."

"Montana, huh? You certainly are a long way from home."

"Yep. And we drove. Well, I could have flown on my broom, but David is scared of flying."

"Cast any spells lately?"

"Nope. We're Presbyterian. We don't cast spells. But Halloween is my favorite holiday. And I have a different color of broom for each day of the week. Of course, we don't have a lot of people out our way. More horses and cows."

"Do any cow tipping?"

"None that I'm willing to admit."

"Are you a part of the home swap group or just checking them out?"

"Is that what this is? I thought this was the Holy Roller Convention. No wonder these people are so subdued. No, we're part of the group."

"What kind of a house do you have?"

"One with a roof, windows, and doors, but we leave them open most of the time. If anyone tries to sneak up on us, the dogs will get them before they get us."

"What kind of dogs do you have?"

"Chihuahuas. Rip a hole in your ankle in nothing flat. They can bite through any kind of boot made. We put them up when we're expecting company. That way we can keep the few friends we have. Of course, if some of them stay too late, I let the dogs out."

"I can't do that with my dog. He'd only want you to rub his tummy. And we keep the duck outside. I'm not sure if it's housebroken, and those feathers would be a pain to clean up."

"I know feathers would be flying if our dogs were around."

I didn't want to think of what might happen to Quiggley if she visited Montana, so I asked them if they knew any of the three couples that I asked the others about. They didn't, so I recommended that Kimberly start taking her medication and moved on. She hit me on my shoulder as I was walking away to let me know that she knew I was kidding.

+++

I found out my next couple was a long way from home too. Bill and Holly Custer. I asked them when their last stand was. They didn't laugh. They must be Baptists. But then they told me they live in Las Vegas. I don't think there are any Baptists in Vegas. I think the Baptists are praying for the people in Vegas though. I just knew that the couple who stood before me didn't look like a couple who took in many of the shows or spent much time in casinos. I figured they saved their money for the collection plate. Yep. Baptists. Baptists put their money in the collection plate and bring lots of food to the potlucks. And they pray a lot. At least that's true of the Baptists I know. Of course, I live in the Bible Belt. Well, a small section of it. I don't know about the ones in Nevada. Those Baptists might be different. Just like the Methodists in California are different from the ones where I come from. I seem to know a lot for a guy who has never been to seminary. I get most of my information from people on Facebook. I've heard they are the most reliable.

I asked the couple standing before me if they knew any of those three couples I had asked others about, but I couldn't see them murdering anyone before or after prayer meeting. But then, years of experience have told me that a lot of the time murderers don't look like murderers. I might have already mentioned that.

+++

I took a moment to check out the room. Most of the people were getting to know other people. There were a couple of knee-slappers and huggers in the group. I guess that meant that someone had just met someone whose house they had stayed in. I guess that meant that both couples had left the house clean when they left and didn't let the dog run away. That last part made me wonder about how Blue would treat someone if they stayed at our place. I mean someone can only do so many tummy rubs. Now the duck is a different story. Not everyone has a pet duck. Would people be willing to share a hot tub with Quiggley?

+++

I wondered if the place where people were standing had anything to do with where they live, because the next couple I introduced myself to lives way west of the Mississippi, just like the others I had just met. And it seemed liked most home-swappers live in the woods. I mean Derek and Annabelle don't, but a lot of the others do.

"Cy Dekker. Kentucky. This is my wife Jennifer. We're trying to meet as many people tonight as we can."

"Well, we're Cheryl and Gordon Walton. We're from the Rocky Mountain State. Colorado."

"I've never been that far west."

"You should come out sometime."

"Someone I met said it was the prettiest state they had been in, and they don't live there."

"We like it."

"That's good because I think people should live where they want. You a part of the group?"

"We are, but we haven't done a lot of swapping. We're new to this and have only been to a few places."

"Where have you been?"

"Well, Gordon has always wanted to go to Florida, so we went there once. That was something else. And we went to New Hampshire once in the fall. And then to California. All three of them were fun trips. We were worn out when we got home, though. Had to rest up from our vacation. Those were long trips. Especially Florida and New Hampshire. We drove. I guess you could say we were rode hard and put up wet."

She laughed when she said that.

"I can understand that. I've been there. Worn out, I mean."

"Have you been to any of those places I mentioned?"

I ignored her question and asked one of my own.

"I wanted to ask you about one of them. Did you by any chance go to Drake and Amanda Peabody's house on Islamorada in the Keys?"

"I think that was their names. It was in the Keys. I know that. Are they here? If they are, I want to meet them."

"No. They couldn't make it this weekend. Something kept them from it."

"Have you stayed at their place?"

"I haven't had the pleasure. I'd love to though."

"It's much better than our place. Not that our place isn't good. But their place was great. Right on the water. And three stories high. The weather was nice while we were there. Plenty of sunshine. And the water was calm. We didn't go out on it, but we did dip our toes in it, so we could say we did. But I did miss my mountains."

I asked them if they knew any of the other couples who were a part of the murder investigation in one way or another, but they said those names were not familiar. I told them it was nice talking to them and moved on to meet someone else.

22

I looked at my watch. We had been there for a while. I wondered how much longer these people would hang around for the four of us to meet them. I wasn't going to waste any time and moved on to meet someone else, someone who had taken a break and moved over to the hors d'oeuvres table. And it wasn't Lou.

"Looks like you have the right idea," I said to break the ice.

They smiled.

"Danny Joe Etheridge. This is my wife, Petrenia."

As soon as he said his name was Danny Joe and the perfect way he said it was enough to let me know this guy was from the south. There are no Danny Joes in New York City. I noticed his wife was cute, and he didn't look too bad. The kind of couple you just knew had good-looking kids and grandkids.

"And I can tell you're from Boston."

They both laughed.

"South Boston," she said. "What gave it away?"

"Well, there are no Danny Joes, Jimmy Joes, and Bobby Joes in North Boston. And I don't think there are any Petrenias anywhere else."

"I can tell you're not from North Boston either."

"Nope. Cy Dekker. Kentucky. My wife is out looking for the restroom."

"She lets you run loose?"

"She tells me to get lost. This way I can tell more lies. You a part of this group?"

"We are and are proud of it. Although I must say that this place has some food that we don't have down home."

"I wasn't sure what some of it was either. Some I ate. Some I told my friend to eat. We're here with another couple. I told him to get lost and spread his lies elsewhere. But we still haven't established if you are from Alabama or Georgia."

"Roll Tide, baby. We don't cotton to them Dogs. But I'm surprised you didn't include Mississippi. They talk right there, too."

"They do at that. I just forgot about them. I meet a lot of Alabama fans when we go to Gatlinburg. We occasionally meet an Auburn fan."

"I didn't realize there were any of them left."

"A few. And there are a lot of Ohio State fans there too."

"We don't mention them Yankees down our way."

"Do you stay in any of their houses?"

"We do, but we wipe the dust from our feet when we leave. But we mostly stay south, go out west, and occasionally head up to New England where they talk funny."

"Want to hear something funny? I once had to act as an interpreter for a Cajun from Louisiana and someone from New Jersey. I'm not kidding. I had to listen closely to understand the Cajun, but then I've had people from Louisiana tell me that some Cajuns are hard to understand sometimes."

"So, why are you here, Cy? Are you one of us?"

I didn't think this was the time to ask them if "us" meant someone who murdered someone, so I said we were there to check out the group, that some friends of ours invited us. I told them about Derek and Annabelle, but they didn't know them. I gave them the other names too.

They didn't know any of them either. I guess none of the three guys I mentioned ever played football for Alabama. I wondered if they noticed that I didn't get any food when I saw Jennifer come back in the door and I left them to join her.

+++

It was only fitting that the next couple we met was from Georgia. I wasn't going to tell them what the Alabama couple said. Especially since she had a cup of coffee in both hands, and I don't think it was the first two she had had since dinner. She told me her name was Debbie Nash and her husband said his name was James. She said I looked familiar. She looked familiar too. I noticed that she was carrying, but as long as she had a cup of coffee in each hand I figured I was safe. She told me she liked NASCAR, and I told her I couldn't understand why men would drive around the same place so many times without stopping and asking for directions. She asked me if I knew who Chapel Hart is, and I asked her if that is where they go to church. She said, "Sometimes."

She told me they live in a large cabin in the woods, and I told her I do too. She thought I was kidding. I told her I don't drink coffee and she offered to pray for me. She asked if I had a dog, and I told her I did. She told me then I couldn't be all bad. I asked her how many dogs she had, and she said, "Dogs are like husbands. One is too many, but it's hard to live without one." Then I asked her again how many she had. She asked, "Dogs or husbands?" Her husband laughed. He was enjoying our conversation, even though he hadn't contributed a word to it.

I found out that they swap houses sometimes when they want to realize how good they have it at home. I asked her if she knew any of the couples I asked everyone about and she told me she didn't. She's a hard woman to tell if she's lying or not. Especially when she's drinking coffee. I expect she is hooked up to an IV filled with coffee when she is sleeping.

+++

I took a chance talking to a woman by herself. It was when Jennifer went to check on Thelma Lou. Jennifer didn't come up behind me and whack me on the side of the head.

"Your husband off by himself?"

"He's so off by himself that I don't have one. Never have had one. Do you have a wife?"

"I've had two. The first one died of cancer much too soon. The second one is fairly recent, and she's wandering around here doing what I'm doing. Meeting people. You're the first single person I've met."

"Well, there are some other single women around here. I've met one or two. By the way, I'm Terri Dubulis from Tennessee."

"I'm Cy Dekker from just north of you. Kentucky. We go to Tennessee a lot. Stay in Gatlinburg. Spend most of our time in Pigeon Forge."

"Know those places well. Are you one of those swappers?"

"Just checking it out. You?"

"Doing the same. Heard about it. Wondering if that's the way I want to travel. So, you don't know any of these people or have heard of any of them?"

"Just the ones I've met here. They seem like nice people. They told me that I don't have to live in a mansion to swap houses. People want to swap to all kinds of places. Even from a big house to a small one."

If she was telling the truth, then she wouldn't know any of the people who have been murdered or discovered someone who had been murdered, but I dropped one name just to see how she would respond. She said it wasn't anyone she had met so far.

+++

People were starting to clear out, but I cornered another couple before they got away. Considering where they live, I doubt if they were cornered a lot.

I approached them. He had on a cowboy hat and boots. I ruled out New York City right away unless his name was McCloud. I figured my best guess was Texas. He took his hat off and scratched his head. I saw that he parted his hair in the middle. It was a big part. A very big part.

"Hi, I'm Cy from Kentucky. If I guess that you're from Texas, would I be far off?"

"I would say you hit the target. I'm Jim Presley and this is my wife, Kaye."

"Did you say Presley?"

"Yes. And we've already heard all the jokes. And while I can sing a little bit, I can't swivel my hips."

"I like his hips," Kaye said, as she joined the conversation. "And by the way, we don't live on South Fork. Wrong part of the state. And we don't know J.R. But we do have a pretty good spread, but nothing like that. Kids and grandkids, and I quilt, and I've been known to teach kids a thing or two over the years."

"I've been trying to teach my wife and my best friend a thing or two and I haven't been able to get to first base. Any suggestions?"

"One. Give up."

"Are you all some of these home swappers?"

"We are. I guess by the way you said that that you aren't?"

"We have some friends who are. That's why we are here. We're checking it out. Another couple, and my wife and me. We're seeing what we can learn. What can you tell me about all this?"

"Some people like it. Some people don't. If you don't, you don't have to keep doing it. It's not a cult."

"Do you by any chance know Derek and Annabelle Oxley, Howard and Gwen Higginbotham, and Drake and Amanda Peabody?"

"Know all of them, in a way."

"Explain what you mean by that."

"Well, we've read some of the Oxleys' books. Because of that, we traded houses with them once. Love their library. We met them for the first time tonight. We've stayed at the Higginbothams too, but we haven't met them. Don't know if they're here or not. We've stayed at the Peabodys too, but, if they're here, we haven't talked to them. Do you know all of them?"

I told them that the Oxleys were friends, that I talked to Howard Higginbotham on the phone once, and I'd seen Amanda Peabody one time at the Oxleys. But the word murder never came up. They said they needed to get back to their room and rest. They didn't sound unnerved. Just tired. I was too, and the only people left to meet I had already met or had spent a lot of time with before I had ever heard of this place.

23

We were so tired when we got through talking to everyone and were no closer to solving the two murders than when we arrived. Jennifer and I decided after we got back to our suite that we would take advantage of room service in the morning and have breakfast in bed.

+++

Not finding the murderer yet was made more palatable when I awoke on Saturday morning and found a lovely creature next to me in bed. I received a second pleasure when there was a knock at the door and breakfast arrived. I got up and answered the door and served Jennifer in bed. We ordered a pastry basket. In addition to that, she decided on bacon and eggs. I opted for eggs Benedict. I had orange juice. She had apple juice.

+++

Lou called while we were eating.
"I'm in the middle of my eggs Benedict," I said.
"And I'm in the middle of today's clue."
"Well, out with it."
"The murderer is here."
"In your suite?"

"No. At Mohonk."

"Is that you being brilliant for a change or today's clue?"

"I'm always brilliant, so it's today's clue."

"I must say you hide your brilliance well. And at least we haven't wasted our time by coming here. I could get used to this place."

"By the way, where are you? We are in the Main Dining Room and I don't see you."

"I am in the middle of my bed, and I'm glad I don't see you. It wouldn't seem as romantic with you here."

"I wish I had thought of that."

"I'm glad you didn't show up."

"I mean ordered breakfast delivered to our suite."

"That's the reason I'm a lieutenant."

"And this is the reason I'll be on time for the meeting."

+++

We took our time eating, then showered, and were a little late joining the others. I took note of the fact that it was theater seating, and we were not the only ones running late. Lou and Thelma Lou were already there, and he patted a seat next to him. We sat down just as someone was approaching the podium.

There were a few welcoming comments, first from someone from Mohonk, then that guy left and someone from the home-swapping group took his place. We were told the session would begin with a few comments, then there would be a time to answer any questions anyone might have, and then a few people would share experiences they have had with home swapping. I didn't expect any of those experiences to be anything about murder, so I only planned to listen with one ear. It wouldn't be long before I wasn't listening with either ear.

Because we were late, and Lou told me they had only arrived a few minutes before Jennifer and I did, we were seated near the back. The chairs were divided into two sections, so there were only six seats on each side with a middle aisle. Lou knew I like to sit on the aisle, so he left the aisle seats for us. There was no one on the other side of Thelma Lou, so the four of us had the row to ourselves.

A few minutes into the festivities, a gentleman entered the room and approached me, and spoke quietly.

"Cy Dekker?"

I nodded.

"Will you and Mr. Murdock come with me?"

I hoped Lou hadn't robbed the safe and left his fingerprints all over it, and they thought with me there, he wouldn't put up as much of a fuss when arrested.

I motioned for Lou to follow me and told Jennifer I had no idea why we were being summoned. Because it was a man and not a woman I was following, she stayed in the room and tried to gather as much information as she could about how home-swapping and murder go together.

Lou and I stepped out into the hall and closed the door. Others were entering as we were leaving and giving us quizzical looks. Some of them were people I had met. People Sam was checking up on or would be checking on soon. We walked a few steps before the man stopped and turned to let us know why we were asked to leave the room. I knew it wasn't because I hadn't showered. Maybe someone had seen how poorly Lou and I had done at the archery range and the tomahawk throw. Maybe they felt we needed lessons about how to do those things more than we needed information about exchanging houses.

"Lt. Dekker, your Chief called us and told us why you are here."

"Is that a problem?"

"No. And please don't interrupt me until I let you know why I called you out of that room.

"I checked up on you and found out that you are one of the best homicide detectives in the country and how you have solved every case you have worked on. I did that because your Chief thought that maybe the murderer would be here this weekend as part of the home swap group. I'm inclined to agree with him. Now.

"There has been a murder here this morning. One of the couples who is a part of that group was found dead this morning by one of our employees. They were found dead in their room. Our local police were informed and have just arrived. They know of your reputation and covet your involvement. I want to take you to the scene of the crime now. Our medical examiner will be arriving momentarily. I think you understand that we want to keep this as hush-hush as we can. Any questions?"

"Not until we get to the scene of the crime."

"One other thing, Lieutenant, Sergeant. We can pinpoint the time of the murder down to ten minutes because the couple was seen leaving the dining room at 9:15 and their bodies were discovered at 9:35. It would take them five minutes to walk from the dining room to their room."

I didn't know if things were going to get better or worse for me. I soon found out one way they were going to get worse.

I asked him for a minute so I could let Jennifer and Thelma Lou know where we were going. He agreed but asked me to do it as quickly as possible and to do it by calling them out into the hall. He didn't want the others to see the looks on their faces when I told them. The look you get when you find out about a murder you don't expect is hard to hide.

+++

Lou and I went off to meet the local authorities while Jennifer and Thelma Lou checked out the faces of the people in the room, to see if any of them looked suspicious. I almost keeled over when I found out who the dead couple was. Karl and Kristin Olsen, the nice couple from Minnesota, would not be doing any more ice fishing. They were probably the nicest couple I had met since we had arrived. I hate it when bad things happen to good people. Especially when they are murdered.

Lou and I walked into the room, and we were introduced. We told the locals about the murder in our jurisdiction in Kentucky and the one in North Carolina and how they were connected.

"Lt. Dekker, unless this was dropped to throw us off, this couple was given a dose of something contained in this syringe, and they died immediately. Whoever did it didn't want them to call for help. Also, this book was found beside where Mrs. Olson fell. Maybe she was getting ready to read, although I would think they were on their way to join the others. We are in the process of checking to see who is a part of that group and doesn't have an alibi for the fifteen-minute period in which the murders were committed. Since you know more about this than we do and are more qualified than we are, we are happy to turn the investigation over to you."

I told them what I knew so far.

"First of all, the book is the murderer's calling card. He or she left it at the scene of one of the other murders. The only reasons the murderer didn't leave it at the other scene are that the victim was found in water, plus the book was written by the two people who live in that house. I think the murderer wants us to know that the book is a clue.

"Also, I met this couple last night. Talked to them for ten or fifteen minutes. They were so nice. I'm not sure, but I suspect that there is some reason why whoever did this chose this couple over any other couple here. I know it wasn't their demeanor. I feel I'm a good judge of character, and I wouldn't have minded this couple being my neighbors or members of my church. Even though I just met them, I'm going to miss them, and Lou and I will work hard to find their killer."

I stood there wondering why this couple was murdered. What set them apart? Or would there be more murders? Did whoever murdered them come here specifically to murder them, or did this person decide on them after he or she arrived? At least I would be able to narrow my suspect list after the locals checked on everyone's alibi.

24

The medical examiner was able to quickly determine the cause of the murders. I would make sure to tell Frank how quickly some MEs were able to come up with the cause of death. Both victims were injected with a poison that killed them instantly in their rooms as soon as they returned from breakfast. They didn't even have time to holler for help.

I was working at the same time the ME was working. Each person attending the home swap weekend checked in, and there was a record of the time each person checked in at the session this morning. I took into consideration the amount of time it took for someone to get from the victims' room to the room where the program was going on and saw who checked in after that time. Several couples could have murdered the Olsons. I hoped most of them had alibis because I didn't want to talk to almost twenty people. As it turned out, there weren't as many people as I thought. Robin McElvain from Texas, Bill and Sue Adams from Kentucky, Jean Sibley from Virginia, Todd and Alisha Collins from South Carolina, June Carter from Kentucky, Martha and Bruce Dollar from Alabama, and Jeff and Randa Hoffman from Wisconsin all had alibis for being late. They were all still eating breakfast in the Main Dining Room at the time of the murders. I wondered if that Carter woman was the one who married Johnny Cash.

That left us with six suspects, two of whom I had met. Anne and Mark Perkins from New Hampshire, and Kaye and Jim Presley from Texas. I hadn't met any of the others; Roger and Clara Thornhill, Mitch Evers and Maggie McKendrick (a married couple, but she still uses her maiden name), Amanda Woods (a young single woman), and Miles Dumont (a young single man). It was time to talk to each of them, one at a time. Each of them was being detained, and husbands were separated from their wives. I decided to start with the ones I had already met.

+++

I began with Mark Perkins.

"We meet again."

"What is this all about?"

"You seemed a little suspicious when I asked you some questions last time."

"I did think you were a little nosy. Maybe that's just your personality. I did like that you introduced us to the Oxleys however. I'm glad they were so nice because Anne and I enjoy reading their books."

"Have you taken their books to heart?"

"I don't understand what you mean by that."

"They write mysteries. About murder and home swapping. Let me explain. I told you that my name is Cy Dekker. What I didn't tell you is that I'm a homicide detective."

"Are you telling me that the Oxleys have been murdered?"

"Not the Oxleys. But someone else has been. Did you by any chance meet Karl and Kristin Olson?"

"From Minnesota? A young couple? Don't tell me they were murdered."

"I'm afraid they were. So, you met them."

"We did. They were one of the nicest couples we met."

"And you have stayed at the Peabodys' home."

"Have they been murdered too?"

"They have."

"But we never met them."

"So you say. I'm not accusing you of anything, but you don't have an alibi for the time the Olsons were murdered."

"When was that?"

"This morning. Before you joined the group."

"We had breakfast brought up to our room. You can check."

"We already have. But we don't know where you were between the time your breakfast arrived and when you showed up where the others had gathered."

"We took our time eating. Then we took our time getting ready. We knew the schedule for this morning. We didn't think we were going to learn anything during the first part of the program. And you won't find our fingerprints on the gun."

"Or anyone else's fingerprints. They weren't shot. Too noisy."

"So they were stabbed or poisoned."

"Very good."

"Well, I can't stand the sight of blood and I don't know anything about poisons."

"We're not accusing you of anything. We have other suspects too."

"So, are we free to leave?"

"What's your hurry? No, you can't leave. But you can move around the property after you are fitted with an ankle bracelet."

When I saw the look on his face, I told him that I was kidding about the ankle bracelet and that if we didn't get any incriminating evidence, they would be able to leave in the morning.

Anne Perkins was the next person I questioned, and she didn't say anything that contradicted anything her husband said. Either they had rehearsed, or they are innocent. It was time to move on to other suspects.

+++

This time the woman came in first. Kaye Presley.

"Howdy again."

"Howdy, yourself," I replied.

"What's going on?"

"It's a home-swapping weekend. I thought you knew that."

"But why do Jim and I have to come and talk to you separately? And why did you take us away from the meeting?"

"We have a question about one of the couples. Karl and Kristin Olson. Have you met them?"

"We did, and I don't think they are the kind of people who would abscond with the silver."

"They say *abscond* in Texas?"

"Not a lot. I think I heard it on TV."

"What can you tell me about them?"

"Not much. They seem like a nice couple. They enjoy home swapping. They said they used to do bed and breakfasts, but they like this better."

"They told me that too."

"So, you've met them?"

"I have. And I don't think they would abscond with the silver. Did you notice anyone talking to them? Maybe someone who didn't seem to like them?"

"I didn't notice them at all, except when Jim and I were talking to them."

"And you told me that you know the Peabodys."

"We don't know them, other than getting a feel for them by staying in their house. We liked their place. But then who wouldn't like a home in the Keys where the weather is great."

"Except during hurricane season."

"I hadn't thought about that."

"What can you tell me about the Peabodys?"

"From the photographs that hung on their walls, they seemed to be a fun-loving couple. They loved to travel, but they seemed to love where they lived. They had pictures of their friends too."

"Did you recognize anyone here in any of those pictures?"

"I didn't look that closely, but I don't think anyone here this weekend is in any of them. I know they loved the water. There were several pictures of the two of them, both alone and with others, with Mrs. Peabody in a bikini and Mr. Peabody in trunks. But they also liked the snow. There were a couple of pictures of them posing on skis."

"Do you know Anne and Mark Perkins?"

"Met them this weekend."

"What is your take on them?"

"They seemed nice. You still haven't told me what this is about."

"I'm a homicide detective. Both the Peabodys and the Olsons have been murdered."

"Here?"

"The Olsons here. The Peabodys' bodies were found in two other homes. Both of those homes were home swap homes. The murderer is someone here."

"You don't think *we* did it?"

"I don't think anyone, in particular, did it. But I'm questioning anyone who doesn't have an alibi for the time of the murder."

"When were they killed?"

"This morning."

"We were tired. We slept in."

"And no one can confirm that."

"Just the two of us."

"There are others who are in the same boat. We are talking to everyone. Feel free to enjoy the resort, but don't leave yet."

She didn't have the look of someone who was going to enjoy the next few hours.

She was ushered out one door and her husband was shown in another. He took off his hat and wiped his forehead.

"What's all of this about?"

"We're talking to a few couples. Some singles too. You just happen to be one of them."

"Why you? Does this have something to do with home swapping?"

"It does in a way. I want to know what you know about Drake and Amanda Peabody and Karl and Kristin Olson?"

"Who?"

"You stayed at the Peabodys' place in the Keys, and you met the Olsons from Minnesota since you got here."

"Oh! Them. I don't know anything about the couple who lives in the Keys except they have a nice place. I've never met them, but I wouldn't mind going back to that house again. I liked that other couple, the one that talks funny. They were a nice young couple."

"What did you talk about?"

"The women did most of the talking. You know how that is. I don't know what they talked about."

"What about the Peabodys? Tell me about your visit there."

"Nice pool. I could probably get used to deep-sea fishing. When it got too hot, I could come back inside. Nice place. I could live there, but I'm a Texan all the way. And it gets hot in Texas too."

"Why were you late this morning?"

"I didn't know we had to be there at a certain time. We were tired. We slept late."

"So, no one can vouch for where you were before you got to the meeting?"

"Why should they?"

"Both the Peabodys and the Olsons have been murdered. You stayed in one house and met the other couple."

"You don't say."

"I do say."

"I would say there are a lot of other people who have done both."

"But most of the others have an alibi for the time of the murders. We're not accusing you of anything. We're checking into everyone who could've done it."

"Well, I couldn't have done it, and neither could my wife."

"Just stick around. We're telling the others the same thing."

+++

I looked at my watch. Time was getting away from me. It was lunchtime. The others could wait until after lunch.

I turned to Lou who had remained silent the whole time. I like him better when he is quiet. Well, most of the time.

"What do you think?"

"I think you've done all of the talking."

"What else do you think?"

"I think we should have turned our wives loose on them. And I think it's time to eat. My stomach told me that a half hour ago."

"I'm surprised you didn't take your M&Ms out and start eating them."

"I did think about calling room service."

"I don't think that would have been a good idea."

"I wasn't going to order anything for the prisoner."

"None of those people are prisoners. Not yet anyway."

Lou and I decided to do our best to create a beautification project and have the girls join us for lunch. We wanted to know if they were able to learn anything in the meeting. Or during the break.

25

We had an enjoyable lunch. Jennifer and Thelma Lou said they would ask Anne Perkins and Kaye Presley to join them at the Tomahawk Toss and have the two of them take turns being a target while our wives shot arrows. If they got a confession, they would let us know to quit grilling the other suspects.

+++

I went back to the grilling room and fluffed my pillow. The next person to be shown in was Roger Thornhill. He was a nice-looking man, graying around the temples.

"Is there something I can do for you? Who are you, anyway? And why did you summon me?"

"I'm Lt. Dekker, a homicide detective. This is Sgt. Murdock. We're here investigating a murder. We're talking to everyone who signed up for the home swap weekend but wasn't on time for the meeting this morning."

"I wasn't on time for any of them. I haven't attended any of the meetings. My name is really George Kaplan. I'm a private investigator. The person who hired me, whose name I'm not willing to divulge, suspected that someone might be murdered here this weekend. I've been floating around the premises when the meetings let out. But I can't be everywhere. You say someone was murdered here this weekend?"

"Two someones. Husband and wife. Can I see some identification?"

"As soon as you show me yours."

Lou and I showed him our credentials, and he showed me something that said he was a private investigator from Albany, New York."

"And the woman with you?"

"Another investigator posing as my wife."

"Are you aware of any previous murders?"

"No. Just that a couple from Minnesota has been threatened. Also, a couple from North Carolina."

"We have two murdered couples. One from each of those states. One was murdered here. The other was murdered somewhere else."

"I haven't seen anyone who seemed suspicious. At least not someone who attended those sessions. I've seen a man and two women that I followed until they disappeared. I never saw any of the three a second time."

"Describe them."

"The man was young and tall. One woman was probably around forty. The other one was quite elderly. All of them seemed to be snooping."

"And you don't know any of the people who are signed up for the home swap?"

"Not by name. Some of the faces are becoming familiar. I've followed some of them around. The ones who looked like they might be up to something."

I didn't know if any of what he said was the truth, but I had no reason to hold him. I would have Sam check on him on Monday. I bid him goodbye and had his coworker come in. Her answers were similar to his. Nothing she said aroused suspicion.

+++

The next person I questioned was Suzy Hendrix. She came in and started talking before she took a seat.

"Before you start your sales pitch, I can tell you that my husband and I talked it over and we've decided that we don't want to be a part of the group. We like this place so well that we want to come back here and go to other resorts like this instead of swapping homes with other couples. My husband was against it from the start. After seeing what this place is like, I've decided to go along with his wishes."

I held up my hands to silence her.

"First of all, let me tell you that I have nothing to do with the home swap group."

"Then who are you, and why did you summon me? And why did you separate my husband and me?"

"First, let me ask you a question. How many sessions have you attended? And how many of the couples who are taking part have you talked to?"

"We walked out on the first one. My husband and I thought what they were doing was silly. And as far as I know, we haven't talked to any of those who trade their homes for a week or more. Why do you ask?"

"I'm Lt. Dekker. My friend here is Sgt. Murdock. We're homicide detectives."

"Well, we're not so much against it that we would murder someone. Is that what's going on? Did someone get killed here this weekend?"

"I'm sorry to say that one of the couples was murdered."

"Well, we didn't do it. We'd have no reason to murder any of them. We don't even know any of them. And no one has done anything to us to make us mad."

I dismissed her and called her husband in. The only difference in their answers was that he did meet two or three people from the home swap group. He went to the Main Dining Room for breakfast a couple of mornings while his wife slept in. He said they were pleasant people. He couldn't remember their names, but he remembered that one couple was from Florida and the other couple was from Missouri.

+++

We had two more people to talk to, a single woman and a single man. The young lady was shown in first. She was the kind of young woman that Jennifer wouldn't want me to talk to, young and attractive.

"Are you police?"

"What made you ask that?"

"Well, are you?"

"We are. Homicide detectives. What made you think we are the police?"

"We might be here for the same reason."

"You're a cop?"

"No. I'm Amanda Woods. My sister was Amanda Peabody."

"Two Amandas?"

"Yep. And our dad said if he had a third daughter, he would name her Amanda too."

"Didn't it get confusing?"

"Nope. They called me AJ. I was Amanda Jo. She was Amanda Lynn. I'm here because I think that whoever murdered my sister and brother-in-law is here."

"Do you know who Karl and Kristin Olson are?"

"No. Should I?"

"They got murdered here."

"Oh no. And they were a part of the group too?"

"And also a young couple. Even younger than your sister."

"My sister wasn't all that young anymore. She just tried to act young. And they lived like they were young. Have you seen the house they lived in?"

"No. But I know where it is. Do you have any leads as to who might have murdered your sister and brother-in-law?"

"No. I just know that their bodies were left in two different places, and they were murdered in two different places."

"How close were you and your sister?"

"As close as two busy sisters can be. We were closer growing up. But we kept in touch at least once a week by phone. And our parents kept us up to date on how the other one was doing. You were probably told that she had no living family. If so, that was done to protect the rest of us. They received death threats, but we don't know who from. If they knew, they didn't tell anyone. My sister wouldn't have wanted me to be following up on this."

"And you shouldn't be. If this isn't your line of work."

"It's not. I'm in real estate. I'm the one who found my sister's home for her. They both loved it. And I think those that stayed in it when my sister and brother-in-law were away loved it too. I don't think it was anyone who swapped homes with them who killed them, but I have no idea who did."

I couldn't think of anything else to ask her, but I would have Sam check up on her to see if she was who she said she was.

+++

One person left and no confession.

The last person came in. Miles Dumont. I couldn't read him. He was either likable or crafty. I wasn't sure which. Of course, he could have been both.

"Are you calling me in to tell me that I won a free week at this place?"

"I'm afraid I don't have the power to do that."

"Then why did you call me in? Did you see me pick that guy's pocket?"

"I did. He wants his handkerchief back or he's going to press charges."

"He can have it. He needs to start washing them every day."

"You were late to the meeting this morning."

"Didn't I tell you? I dropped out."

"So, where were you?"

"Did we have a date or something?"

"No. But you were late, and that's why we have one now."

"Are you talking about that home swap thing?"

"Isn't that why you came?"

"Not really. I came to meet babes. I saw some, but they didn't interest me."

"They turned you down, huh?"

"I was more interested in seeing this place than joining that group. To tell you the truth, I don't even have a home to swap."

"Did you meet any of those people?"

"A few. At dinner. At the pool. And shooting arrows. One of those women was very good at that. I wouldn't want to cross her."

"Do the names Amanda Peabody or Amanda Woods mean anything to you?"

"Amanda Woods does. I loved *The Holiday*."

"What about Kristin Olson?"

"Was she one of the characters in *Little House on the Prairie*? That was before my time."

"No. She wasn't."

"Did you see anyone following anyone else or threaten anyone else?"

"No. Can't say that I did. Why? Did someone complain?"

"Not that I know of."

I wasn't sure if he was being serious or playing with me. I just knew he either wasn't guilty, or if he was, I wasn't going to get a confession out of him. I would put him on Sam's list with the others. I told him to have a good day and sent him on his way. I think he left not knowing why he was summoned in the first place.

26

As I was walking out the door to find my wife, a woman bumped into me.

"Oh, sorry, Cy," she said, then seemed embarrassed and hurried away.

I was taken by surprise, and she was fifteen or twenty feet away before I thought to see who it was. I didn't recognize her, but all I had was a view of her back. As best I could tell, she looked to be around forty or so and had dark blonde hair. She looked nothing like the woman who bumped into me before. Didn't sound like her either. What is it with women bumping into me in the hallway and knowing who I am? And I have no idea who they are.

"Lou, who was that?"

"No one I've seen before."

As always, not recognizing someone bothered me. But I put it aside and went to see if Jennifer had discovered the murderer's identity while I questioned those who might have done it.

+++

Jennifer didn't have anyone in handcuffs when I caught up with her. Neither did Thelma Lou, but then Thelma Lou is timid about such things.

The four of us took a walk down to the lake. We found a spot where we could spot someone sneaking up on us before they could inject us with poison or throw a tomahawk that would hit any of our body parts. Jennifer said that no one got rowdy during the session, which mainly consisted of people getting up and giving testimonials of how much they enjoyed other people's homes and answering questions newbies or those considering giving it a try might have about swapping homes or toothbrushes. That's pretty much what I expected. I was beginning to wonder if the murderer was even in that room. But then today's clue said the murderer is here. But then that was obvious. It's hard to inject someone long distance. I was frustrated. I didn't even have any top-notch suspects.

"Cy, after you told me what was going on when Thelma Lou and I came back into the room, we switched over to the other side of the room so we could keep an eye on anyone peeping in the door. We didn't see anyone. Did you learn any more about the dead couple or whoever might be responsible?"

"It depends on which dead couple you're talking about."

Jennifer gave me a quizzical look.

"I questioned six people or couples. Two of them were people we had met during one of the Meet and Greet times, who didn't try to kill us in front of an audience. One of the others claimed to be the sister of the dead woman who didn't make it this far, the one we found at Derek and Annabelle's house, and one of the guys said he is a private detective. But he didn't seem to be all that good of one. One of the others claimed they decided shortly after they got here that they aren't interested in home swapping, and they walked out of the first Meet and Greet before it started. The only difference between the husband's answers and his wife's answers is that he claims he went to breakfast a couple of times while she slept in. The single guy claims he just came to meet women and was disappointed in the single women he had seen. When Sam gets back from whatever he is doing this weekend, I'll have him check up on all of them to see if they check out. At this moment, they seem to be the only suspects we have. I have a feeling that about half of them aren't telling the truth, but I'm not sure if one of them is the murderer or not. But I'm not sure what other reason they would have for lying to me."

"In other words, like in most other cases, so far you don't have much to go on."

"I wish you hadn't put it that way, but yeah."

A breeze came up from over the water. It felt good. A lot better than the case felt. I wondered when the Chief was going to come to his senses and find someone younger to take over. Lou and I could always advise them. Well, I could.

I stopped thinking about the case and took in the view. The lake, the trees, the large structure where we were staying, and someone was murdering. Yeah, it was hard to keep my mind off the case.

It was only Saturday. Late afternoon, but still Saturday. It wouldn't be long before we would be heading to dinner. I wondered where the murderer would be heading. But would I be spinning my wheels until Sam came back from wherever he was spending the weekend? There isn't much I can do until Sam checks out our six suspects. I wouldn't feel guilty enjoying the resort. I wondered where Derek and Annabelle were. I wasn't going to share that thought with Jennifer.

I figured most of the home swappers would be staying until morning, then checking out. Would they be safe after they checked out? One couple was murdered in someone else's home. The other was murdered not far from where I sit. The murderer is unpredictable. That makes everything harder.

+++

We stayed a few more minutes enjoying the lake setting and then walked back up to where the murderer might be lurking. It was time to get ready for dinner. I told our neighbors we would meet them in the lobby. Somehow, probably with Thelma Lou's help, Lunkhead found the lobby and behaved himself while we ate. After we finished our six desserts, the one I ate and the five more I dreamed of eating, I told the others I wanted some time alone to mull over the case. Actually, that wasn't the truth. But I wasn't off to meet another woman.

Before I mentioned anything to anyone else, I needed some time to mull over how I was going to waste my Sunday. I was used to going to church, eating out, and taking a nap. One of those wouldn't be happening where I would be in the morning.

I perused my options. I quickly disposed of anything having to do with water other than drinking it. Rowboating, paddleboating, kayaking, canoeing, paddleboarding, and fishing didn't seem like something that would have a good ending for me. I would recommend them to Lou instead. If I could get Jennifer to show me how to take a video of Lou on a board on the water, I think some money could be made on YouTube. And if I tried the indoor pool, there was a much greater chance that you know who would show up instead of Annabelle. It's bad enough that he lives next door to me. I've seen him make a crash landing into his hot tub. He calls it his swan dive. It looks more like an ugly duckling. But enough of that.

Golf. I've tried that torture. I remember the time I thought it might be fun. I even did it a couple of times a week for a few weeks. Without Lou finding out about it. One time I hit a ball off the tee, and it landed on the green. I had never done that before. I didn't know what club to use next. I decided on a sand wedge. It turned out to be the right club, because I hit it properly, didn't make a divot on the green, and the ball landed within ten feet of the green I was aiming for in the first place. I can picture myself trying to play golf here. Cy slices the ball into the trees. It lands right next to the murderer. Cy is found a few days later with his head bashed in and his five-iron next to him. Scratch that one too.

Spa and Wellness. Yeah. Right. Jennifer isn't going to let some other woman touch my body. And they have an exercise that involves huge balls. I don't know if you are supposed to sit on them and bounce around or what. If I did that, I would fall off and break something or other. The something or other would be one of my bones. Cross that one off my list too. That is another thing I can recommend to Lou, if he survives the lake. Bouncing balls and some woman mutilating his body. He might like the second one, if Thelma Lou, Frank, and George never found out. Of course, if I knew, they would find out.

I've already ridden in the carriage, and that was fun. But once is enough. And I'm not going to try to climb up on a horse, so the stables are out. And the horses will thank me for that.

Outdoor adventures. I've had all of those I want. I've walked all I want, and I'm not climbing rocks or rock walls. Time to move on again.

Tennis. The only kind of tennis I do is table tennis. Maybe they have a ping-pong table. Maybe Lou and I could watch Jennifer and Thelma Lou play tennis.

I finally saw one thing I could do. Corn Hole. I didn't realize they play it this far north. But then, I can do that at home. If I know Jennifer, she is probably somewhere else, thinking about what we will do tomorrow, and she has already signed me up for a rock-climbing class.

Just as I thought of her, here she came. Bad timing, because at the same time, another woman came walking by.

"Hi, Cy."

Jennifer didn't believe me when I said I didn't know who she was, but I really didn't know her. I had never seen her before. And she didn't look anything like any of the other women who spoke to me. I wondered if my picture was posted on a wall somewhere. I was about to get in trouble for something I didn't do or think.

"Thelma Lou and I are going to try tossing tomahawks tomorrow. Want to come along?"

The only question I could think of that I would like to answer less than that one was, "Does this outfit make me look fat?" Even though Jennifer doesn't look fat in anything, she wouldn't believe me if I said no. She would think I was thinking of how Annabelle would look in the same outfit.

27

Lou and I decided not to join Jennifer and Thelma Lou as they threw tomahawks. Neither scenario I envisioned sounded good to me. Either they would beat anything Lou and I did, or their tomahawks would slip and send one of us to the hospital. We convinced them how important it was for Lou and me to mull over the case. Jennifer asked me if I would be mulling in bed. I told her that I might nap in bed, but I would be mulling somewhere else. I refrained from telling her it would be in a porch rocker with my name on it. I consider myself one of the world's best mullers. Even though I realized that mulling would be as painful as tossing tomahawks. My list of suspects, whom I was fairly certain had murdered someone recently, was so lacking that I considered adding the tomahawk target to it. I know. My brain was taking a break.

I knew that part of my day I would be doing what I do best. Breakfast and lunch. I would put napping before I mulled, but sometimes I snore and wake myself up before I'm ready to face the world again.

Well, Sunday morning arrived. We went to the Main Dining Room, and I looked to see if I saw anyone with four notches in his or her belt. Or if anyone there looked like they were guilty of any recent murders. Or didn't have as many copies of *Bad Swap* as they arrived with. No one there noticed me. Well, some did, but none of them spilled their coffee or juice when I made eye contact. Of course, there was a good chance the murderer had finished here and was off to leave books in other locations. If so, that could present a problem.

+++

We parted ways after breakfast and Lou and I headed to the nearest rockers. He saw which one I was headed for and tried to slide in under me before I could sit down. I was too quick for him. Luckily, no one else was there to notice. Lou was aware of that too, so he didn't whisper in my ear.

"Cy, think outside of the box."

"We have a box?"

"No. We have a clue."

"And the clue is 'Think outside of the box?'"

"You're improving."

"What does it mean?"

"It means to find out who murdered these four people."

"That's what I already planned to do. So, whoever murdered them didn't do it in a box. Is that right?"

"Maybe *you* should be in a box."

"It would be too cramped. How about you trying it and letting me know how it is?"

"Cy, do you have any idea who did it?"

"I'm pretty sure it was the murderer. Don't you agree?"

"I'm not sure about you."

"You don't like it when I act like you, do you?"

"I don't act that way."

"Let's just try to figure out what the clue means and which people we can rule out. Or we can wait until Sam rules some of them out."

"I vote for the second one. When does he get back? In two weeks?"

"Sometime today. But we can go ahead and think. Well, at least I can go ahead and think. You can join your wife and Jennifer and offer to be their target."

+++

If we counted each couple as one, we had six suspects. Anne and Mark Perkins, Kaye and Jim Presley, Roger Thornhill, Suzy Hendrix, Amanda Woods, and Miles Dumont. I wasn't sure if any of them looked or acted like they were more guilty than the others. And some of them said they were related or detectives. Sam would tell me if that was true. I looked at my watch. It wasn't even noon yet. It was too early to call Sam.

Did outside the box mean the murderer wasn't a home swapper? If so, that would let out the Perkins, the Presleys, and the Hendrix. That would leave us with Roger Thornhill, or was his name George Kaplan, who said he was a detective. Also, Amanda Woods, who said she was Amanda Peabody's sister, and Miles Dumont, who said he came to meet babes. I can think of a lot better places to go to meet women. Unless you want to meet rich women. It costs a lot of money to stay at the Mohonk Mountain House, even though it sounds kind of honky-tonk. Or does it mean the murderer is someone we haven't even considered?

We rocked, but we didn't roll. Thankfully. We also didn't solve the case. I was anxious to find out if any of our suspects had flown the coop. I went to the front desk to check. They had been informed who I was and what I was doing from this point on. They checked on my suspects. None of the people I mentioned had flown the coop. All of them had driven away. Well, in a manner of speaking. Some of them hadn't stayed there in the first place. Only the Perkins, the Presleys, and the Hendrix had been registered in the first place. Well, the others were listed as day guests. They paid a few hundred less to roam around. They didn't have to pay a thing to be interrogated by me. I did that pro bono. I do things like that out of the goodness of my heart. That meant that I, or someone of high or low esteem, would have to hunt someone down as soon as we determined who needed to be hunted. Since all of them left, that meant the innocent left, as well as the guilty.

+++

After the girls had thrown their arms out of joint and had showered and reapplied their deodorant, they joined Hilldale's finest (and Lou) for lunch. We didn't dare ask them how they did. That way they didn't have to lie or brag. Or take us back to where they had gotten rid of all of their stress and demonstrate for us.

+++

After what I determined was a reasonable amount of time, I called Sam. He said he was within a thousand miles of Hilldale on his way home. Two things kept me from believing him. One was that I knew he wouldn't go anywhere one thousand miles away from home. And two, I recognized the sound of his refrigerator door closing.

"Your car has a refrigerator now, does it?"

"That's my limo driver."

"Oh good. That means your hands are free to write down the names of today's suspects."

"You know how the economy is these days, Cy. Limos don't come with pencils."

"Just bleed and use your finger."

After I gave him all of the names, he did something that was very unSam-like.

"Is that all of them?"

"I cleared all of the others while you were playing."

"So, there were only six suspects, to begin with."

"Just get back to me within an hour so I can wrap this up and head for home."

+++

"So, girls, what activity are you going to tackle next?"

"Thelma Lou and I are going to challenge you and Lou to a paddleboard race."

"In our suite?"

"On the lake. Or would you prefer the kayak flip?"

"Lou told me he's interested in all of that, but I have to wait here until Sam calls me back to let me know which one of our suspects is the murderer."

"Is this the same Sam I know?"

"One and the same."

"Good. Because it will be tomorrow before he will call. You know how slow Sam is. Besides, this is Sunday. Sam is like Hobby Lobby and Chick-fil-A. He takes Sundays off."

"Sam takes every day off. But somehow, he stumbles into a few things that help me."

"I admit you need a lot of help. But Sam won't be providing that until tomorrow. And probably not early. When did you give him the names of the suspects? You didn't know about the murder until yesterday."

"A few minutes ago."

I didn't have to do anything that involved drowning, but Jennifer and Thelma Lou lassoed us into doing something with them. Something that didn't involve me dying before I solved the case.

28

I didn't know what we would have to do next or where we would have to go to do it, so the four of us stayed another night at the resort. We also decided to sleep in and have breakfast in our suites. I had finished my time with God and my shower, and I was spending a few minutes out on the balcony looking at some of God's creation when the phone rang. It was some guy back in Hilldale by the name of Sam.

"Cy, you may or may not like the news I have for you."

"That means you don't have the name of the murderer for me."

"Cy, are you losing it, or could you by some chance be playing tricks on me?"

"As far as I know, neither one of those is true. Why do you ask?"

Well, I've cleared the Perkins and the Presleys. At least for the first two murders. They couldn't have done them. They had alibis."

"Nothing unusual about that. You've found people with alibis before."

"But before, when you gave me names of people, they existed."

"The Perkins and the Presleys exist. I've talked to them more than once."

"I'm not talking about any of them. I'm talking about the other four. Did they come together?"

"I don't think so. I never saw any of them together. Why do you ask?"

"Because none of them are real people."

"All of them are real people. I talked to them. They talked to me. They didn't walk through doors. They had to open the door to enter and leave the room."

"I'm sure that's true, Cy. That's not what I'm talking about."

I went on as if he hadn't spoken.

"One of them even showed me his driver's license and ID that showed me that he is a Private Detective."

"Well, if he is, he lied to you about his name. I can tell you this much. I can tell you where everyone got his or her name. Roger Thornhill is a character played by Cary Grant in Alfred Hitchcock's *North by Northwest*. George Kaplan was a made-up character in that same movie who didn't even exist in that movie. Sam and Suzy Hendrix were characters played by Efrem Zimbalist Jr. and Audrey Hepburn in the movie thriller *Wait Until Dark*. Amanda Woods was a character played by Cameron Diaz in the movie *The Holiday,* and Miles Dumont was a character played by Jack Black in the same movie. Surely those two were working together."

"If they were or are, none of us picked up on it, and I've even seen that movie. I even liked it."

"So, you don't know these people's real names, Cy?"

"Not only that, but some of them were also only day guests here. They never had a room here, so who knows where they are now."

"Do you know if they were fingerprinted?"

"I don't. But I will find out. I doubt if they were. I don't see why they would have been. After all, we questioned quite a few people."

"Is there anyone else who is real that I can run down for you?"

"No. Just find my escapees."

Sam laughed and then hung up.

I informed the others where we stood. Did we let the murderer slip through our fingers? We did. But was it one of these four, or someone else?

+++

All of us found a comfortable place to sit. It was time to mull over the case together and see what we were forgetting.

I went out onto the balcony but blacked out everything that was in front of me. It wasn't too hot, and there was a breeze, but I tried not to think about that. I merely wanted to solve the case and move on to something a lot more fun.

I sat down and thought back to the beginning, all the way back to where Amanda Peabody's body was discovered in Derek and Annabelle's pool. Nothing there rang a bell, but I remembered that Joey told me about a woman getting out of a car. There must have been a second person in that car because someone drove a couple of houses down the street and stopped. But Joey didn't see the woman go to the Oxley's house, nor did he see anyone get out of the car. Maybe whoever that was had nothing to do with Amanda Peabody's murder. But it was something to keep in mind. Or was it?

Did thinking outside the box mean that whomever the murderer was meant that the murderer was never in the room with the home swappers? Or wasn't one of the home swappers? Thinking about all of this was making my head hurt, and I was just starting to think about it.

Lou must have known that I was getting nowhere, because I heard the sliding glass door open, and there he was.

"Cy, I got a second message. God must know that we're getting nowhere trying to solve this murder."

"I'm sure God knows. He knows everything. But I don't. So, what's the message?"

"You can tell a person by what's on their plate."

"I agree. Let's go eat."

"It's not time to eat."

"It's always time to eat. What does it mean, anyway?"

"Cy, it means you're supposed to eat poisonous mushrooms and rely on God to save your life."

"God gave you the message. You eat them first."

You can tell a person by what's on their plate. What does that mean? If two people are eating the same thing, how can you tell them apart? Does it mean the way they eat?

"Lou, go back and tell God that you are ready for the third clue of the day."

"I don't think we are supposed to tell God things."

"Then go back and tell Him that both of us are mentally challenged and ask Him for the third clue of the day. And tell Him just in case, would He please throw in clues four and five for good measure."

"I'm going back inside."

"That's good, Lou. Then go into the closet and pray and ask God for however many clues He thinks it will take us to solve the case."

"God already knows how many clues it will take. He knows everything."

"Okay. Go to Plan B."

"What's Plan B?"

"Tell Jennifer the clue and ask her what it means."

"How long should I wait afterward before I come back to tell you the answer?"

"Wait at least fifteen minutes. Anything less and my ego will suffer greatly."

Things were improving. Lou left and I had a box and a plate to ponder. I tried to sneak a peek to see if Jennifer gave Lou the correct answer, but I didn't see her. Then I saw and heard Lou knocking on the bedroom door. I moved along the balcony until I could see into the bedroom. Jennifer was reclining on the bed. She sat up when Lou knocked. From their reaction, I don't think Jennifer gave Lou an immediate answer. That made me feel better about being stupid.

+++

After getting nowhere in record time, I figured that maybe I could stimulate my brain by taking a walk. I was sure that no one I had met who didn't work there was still there. So, I doubted if the murderer was going to open a door and bop me over the head, then pull me into a room and put a book I had already read under my arm. However, just in case, I walked down the middle of the corridor.

I encountered someone delivering room service coming out of a room.

"Excuse me, but I'm trying to solve a riddle, and I'm wondering if you can help me."

"I'll try, but I'm not good at those things."

"You can tell a person by what's on their plate."

"Since I deliver room service, it could be what they leave on their plate that they don't eat. But I'm not sure if it means they aren't hungry or they didn't like what they left on the plate."

I wasn't sure that was the right answer, but I thanked him and walked on.

I tried a concierge in the lobby, but he too was as stumped as I was.

I saw a bellman had no car to unload, so I stepped outside to ask the same question of him.

"I'm always out here unloading one car, truck, van, or SUV after another. So, I notice where people are from. Maybe it's their license plate. You can tell something about a person by what's on their license plate."

That made more sense than what anyone else had to say.

"I think you might have solved my riddle. I slipped him ten dollars for doing nothing except what was important to me and headed back to the room.

I burst into the room and hollered loud enough to wake everyone, even though no one was asleep.

"I think the walk did me good. I'm pretty sure I solved the last clue. I think the plate is a license plate. Maybe we can tell who everyone is by looking at their license plate."

"Didn't their license plate leave when they did?"

"I don't know. Let's check."

29

I dashed out of there like a skunk was on my tail. Or maybe it was only a porcupine. In any case, I was in a hurry, and I didn't want to hear bad news.

I got to the front desk and sought someone with the knowledge and authority to help me.

"Do you have the license plate numbers of everyone who stayed here over the weekend?"

"Let me know why you ask, and I might be able to help you."

"It might help us find the murderer."

"I can give you the license number of everyone who stayed here, but as soon as the police arrived after the murder, they posted a camera at the edge of our property so that they could identify every vehicle that left here. They also had someone down at the dock to make sure no one left by boat. Someone could still cut through the woods, but by it being a camera and not an officer, a person leaving would have no idea that they would be identified. We have a picture of every vehicle that left here. If the person who owned said vehicle stayed here, you can match them with our records. If not, you will have to find that out on your own. A higher camera took a picture of the driver, so you will have a face to go by."

I wanted to do my victory dance, but instead, I kept myself in check and asked another question.

"Can we start working on that list now?"

"I can fix you up a room where you can do just that."

I called Sam to let him know that I would be feeding him a list of people to check on a few at a time. I would include a picture in case he was interested in getting to know any of them. He was so excited that if he had been there, he would have kissed me. Not.

+++

The pictures helped me eliminate any of them whom I recognized that had already been cleared as suspects. There were nearly four hundred vehicles altogether. People in management helped me to eliminate those who worked there who couldn't have committed either of the first two murders.

I sent Sam pictures and license plates ten at a time. He was so grateful that I expected to find a fruit basket in my room by the time I got back to it.

By the time the four of us finished going through all the people who drove away since the murder, as well as those who were still there who had arrived before the murder, there were sixty-seven people left for Sam to check on. If some of them were without an alibi after Sam got back to me, I would have the police check to see if those people were at home, and if not, put out an APB to find where they are.

+++

As soon as the four of us finished going through all the license plates and pictures, I wanted to go through all of them myself. I wanted to see the pictures of the ones I hadn't seen. None of the women whom I had run into or the two guys I saw with a copy of the book were in the pictures I looked through. And none of our four suspects whose names I didn't know were there either. I wanted to make sure they didn't slip through our fingers.

I told the others they could go back to our suites and rest, while I looked at the pictures I hadn't seen. Jennifer stayed with me, while Lou and Thelma Lou headed to their jacuzzi. I wanted to do the same. Well, not to their jacuzzi, but to mine. But I want to make sure the murderer doesn't get away.

I took my time and looked at every one of the pictures I hadn't seen. Some were easy to identify. Some were not. But I felt I could identify the people I was looking for. I finally found each of our suspects, but not either of the two women who called me by name or the old lady named Maggie. I didn't find either of the two men who had a copy of *Bad Swap* either. Not the one who was following me and disappeared into the woods, or the one who was thumbing through the book while sitting on a rocker on the porch. Yet they were there on the property. Had they gotten away before the cameras were installed? The three women looked nothing alike. And they were of different ages. One appeared to be around thirty, one between forty and fifty, and one somewhere around eighty. I saw all of them before the Olsons were murdered. The two guys looked nothing alike either. Maybe they left before then. They might have still been here when the murder was committed. They could have left a day or two before. But then I'm not sure I can identify the guy who followed me if he was standing in a lineup.

+++

Sam got back to me with answers the same way I got possible suspects for him. A little at a time. I was mainly interested in the four people who gave me fake names. I wondered who they really are, and why they lied to me. Surely, all of them aren't murderers. Were some of them criminals of some other type? I wasn't going to drive all over the country, so I decided to wait until after I heard back from Sam about each of the people who left in a vehicle. I hoped our murderer didn't leave on foot, heading through the woods. I guess I should have brought Blue and Quiggley with me for rugged surveillance. But then who am I kidding? Blue wouldn't have been any good at apprehending anyone. And Quiggley would have headed for the water.

+++

Waiting on Sam's final list of people who could have committed the murders gave me time to think about the three women and two men who seemed to disappear, and the four people who gave me fake names. They were not all in on it together. I was pretty sure the murders were the actions of one person or one couple. Were those first five still around when the Olsons were murdered? I knew the ones who lied about who they were were still around. They were there when I questioned them. Why did they lie about who they were? I had no idea. Was the one guy really a detective? Maybe he lost his license and was working for someone under an assumed name. And was the woman really the sister of the first murdered woman, the one found in Derek and Annabelle's pool? If not, did she know her? If none of that is true, why was she here? Especially if she isn't the murderer. Did someone hire her to find out what happened to the real Amanda?

+++

Because sixty-seven is a whole lot of people to track down, Sam wasn't finished identifying everyone and seeing if they had an alibi for the first set of murders by the time we went to bed that night. That was fine with me. I could wait to work. As long as I didn't have to play some kind of water sport. I was hoping that all but one person had an alibi. I did lie awake for a while wondering why one person said she was the victim's sister if she wasn't, and why another person said he is a private detective if he isn't. Those things can be checked. Maybe they didn't think we would check. I quit thinking about all of them when Jennifer noticed that I wasn't asleep, and she turned over and kissed me.

30

It was just before noon when Sam called the next morning with my final suspects.

"Cy, I've made it easy on you."

"You picked up the murderer and he or she confessed?"

"No. I narrowed the list of people with no alibi for the time of the first two murders from sixty-seven to sixty-four. Now, all you have to do is round them all up."

"I know you're kidding. How many are there?"

"If you would look at the e-mail I sent you, complete with a picture of each possibility, you would already know. There are five who could have murdered all four of them. Look at the pictures first and tell me if any of them look familiar to you."

"I don't know how to do that and talk to you at the same time. Let me call you back in a couple of minutes."

"Cy, you don't even know how to find your e-mail? Have someone help you, then call me back. But not with any more suspects. I'm through with this case."

Sam was right. I did need help. I went into the other room and had Jennifer help me. Lou and Thelma Lou had just knocked on the door That meant they could look at the pictures too. Four sets of eyes are better than one. Well, slightly better in this case.

I looked at the first one. Ellie Franklin. Formerly known as Amanda Woods, movie character, and sister of Amanda Peabody. Not only was her name not Amanda, but she didn't live in California. She lives in Pennsylvania. A person who lies about everything is certainly a possibility to be a murderer. The only thing she didn't lie about was her face. It was the same one I questioned. Well, she didn't lie about selling real estate. She is a realtor. Would she be jealous of people who swap homes? I can't see why. But then why would she lie about who she is, and how did she even know about Amanda Peabody? But then she said no one knew Amanda had a sister.

I couldn't tell for sure, but the second person could be the guy who was following us when Jennifer and I went for our walk. He darted into the trees quickly, but I think he's the guy. His name is Brandt Jordan and he's from Tennessee. Evidently, he wasn't at home during the time of any of the murders and was where I was over the weekend. And he couldn't be tracked to any location during that time. And he did have a copy of the book when he was following us.

I didn't recognize the third person, Barb Linkenfelter, from Vermont. She looked to be somewhere around forty-five or so. She didn't look like any of the three women I encountered who seemed to know me. It says she owns a bed-and-breakfast in Vermont. Could she be jealous enough of home-swappers to murder some of them? I doubt if murdering a few of them would hurt her business that much. But then, if she couldn't be found during the time of the murders, maybe business is bad.

The next picture was a picture of a man. Donnie Jo Armstrong. A home swapper. But not someone who swapped homes with anyone who was here over the weekend. I wonder why. It couldn't be because of where he lives. He lives in Georgia. I met people over the weekend from Georgia and states near Georgia. If he hadn't swapped with any of this group, why was he here?

Four down and one to go. The last one was Darrell Bradshaw. A man who lives in an RV. He has no place of residence. He travels all the time. I would think that Sam could have tracked him to wherever he put down roots each night. He must not have stayed in an RV park.

I still couldn't find any of the three women who seemed to know me, and I couldn't find the old lady, Maggie. And I couldn't find one of the men.

It was time to call Sam back.

+++

"Cy, did it take you that long to find someone to help you turn your phone on?"

"You know I know how to turn it on. I was talking to you a few minutes ago. Then I was studying the pictures and reading what little there was about each person."

"Did you recognize any of the people?"

"I know I recognized one of them, and I think I recognized another one."

"You think. I know I couldn't send them to Olan Mills and pick out the best photos to send you, but I did what I could. So, you recognized one of the women."

"How did you know?"

"I know you, Cy."

"It was because I had a sit-down question-and-answer session with her. It turns out that she didn't give the right answers."

"Which one was it?"

"Ellie Franklin. She told me her name was Amanda Woods and she was Amanda Peabody's sister."

"Cy, most people don't give two sisters the same name. Brothers either, except on one TV show."

"She addressed that. She said if her parents had had another daughter, they would have named her Amanda too. Besides, she said her parents called her AJ, not Amanda."

"Sounds like she's a good liar. Or she could be Amanda Woods after all. Do you realize how many Amanda Woods there are in the country? I don't, and I'm not going to check."

"I don't want you to check. She was convincing. Now I have to figure out if she's a murderer. What else can you tell me about her?"

"Only that she sells real estate in Pennsylvania, but she hasn't spent much time there lately. She was in the Florida Keys about the time the first couple left there. I can only find one place in Ohio and one place in North Carolina where she gassed up and spent the night about the time of the first two murders. After that, she went home for a couple of days, then up to where you are. She is now back home in Pennsylvania, showed a house yesterday as a matter of fact. At least she told you the truth about being in real estate. Maybe she wants to sell you a house someday."

"She said she sold the one in the Keys to her sister. That would be easy enough to check. I might want you to check on that if something doesn't break soon."

"Don't do me any favors. Although that wouldn't be hard to find out."

"The other one that I might have seen was a guy who was following me carrying a book that was found beside the bodies of three of the four victims."

"Maybe he wanted to know if you are a reader. Which guy was it?"

"Brandt Jordan."

"The Tennessee guy. I couldn't find much on him. What I found interesting is that he switched vehicles four times during the time the murders took place. I don't know where he works or if he works. I couldn't find anywhere that he rented a motel room. For all I know, he slept in whatever vehicle he was driving or in the woods somewhere. He was the hardest one for me to track. He didn't stay where you stayed, but he drove out of there after that second couple was murdered. He was one of the first ones to leave after the police put their cameras up. And he was in the vicinity of where the first two bodies were found. I think. It was hard to keep up with him the way he kept switching vehicles. And he always chose one that blended in. Although it was always an SUV. What about the others?"

"What can you tell me about Barb Linkenfelter?"

"That she owns a B&B in Vermont, that she closed it down for three weeks and just got back and reopened it. There is nothing strange about that. She did the same thing around this time last year."

"Were there any murders of people of a certain group during the time she was gone last year?"

"I checked on that. I couldn't find any."

"How's her business?"

"She's busiest in the fall. That's when most people go to Vermont. She volunteers in the area, works in a small shop there when she has time, and is involved with the Actors Guild doing whatever they ask her to do. She isn't married, but she goes out to dinner with a couple of the men in the area. No harm has come to either one of them."

"I bet they aren't home swappers."

"No, they are not."

"What about Donnie Jo Armstrong?"

"The Georgia guy. He travels quite a bit during good weather. He was near all of the areas where murders were committed. He sets up a table at flea markets. He seems to enjoy that. He meets people there. Some of them are from out of town and he goes to visit them. Most of the ones he goes to visit are single women, but he does visit some couples. I don't mean he stays with them, but he visits them and takes them to dinner. He inherited a lot of money a few years back, so he's not hurting for money. He has a large home, and he is involved in home swapping, but he has never swapped houses with anyone who was up where you are right now. I'm not sure why he even went there. He left there and headed to Maine. When he's traveling, he never seems to stay in one place for more than three or four days. I don't know when he got to where you are, but he was there. They got his license plate and picture when he left."

"Tell me about the last one, Sam."

"Darrell Bradshaw, character extraordinaire. He lives in an RV and is constantly moving about the country. I don't know why he was where you are, because he didn't stay there, and he has no interest in home swapping since he doesn't own one. Unless you call his RV a home. I couldn't find an address for the guy. I know he has no use for home swapping, hotels, motels, or B&Bs. I did find someone who knows him who said he is hard to get along with and if he sees him again in ten years that is too soon.

"That's about all I can tell you about these people, Cy, unless you have some questions. But I doubt if I can answer them."

"Which one of them murdered these four people?"

Sam laughed.

"Ask Jennifer. Maybe she can help you. Isn't she the one who usually solves your cases?"

"Don't tell anyone, Sam. It's supposed to be a secret."

I thanked him for his help and ended the call.

+++

I turned to the others. Sam's call had been on speaker, so they heard what I heard.

"Do any of you have any ideas as to who the murderer is?"

Lou waved his hand frantically. I was sure he had a stupid remark to make.

"Go ahead, Lou. Get it over with."

"The victims already told you who murdered them."

"Was this last night or this morning?"

"I assume before they were murdered."

"They didn't tell you that?"
"They didn't tell me anything. That is today's clue."

31

Author's Note: You have been given several clues as to who murdered the four people, some of them early in the book. Have you figured it out?

I tried to figure out what today's clue meant. I didn't talk to the Peabodys while they were still alive, and I didn't see Amanda Peabody until she had been pulled from the pool. All I knew about her husband's murder is what Lt. Dinwiddie told me over the phone. He was lying on a couch with a book tucked under his arm. Was that only to let me know that the murders were connected? We would have learned that soon enough. Was it to cast suspicion upon Derek or Annabelle? I didn't think so. I moved on to the Olsons. The nice young couple. I did talk to them. Some of the other couples admitted to talking to them too, including two of the couples we questioned. Could that have something to do with it? Or could it have been something Joey saw, like the woman who visited their house? Only one of the two suspects fit the age range of the woman who visited the house one night. That was the woman who claimed she was Amanda Peabody's sister. The woman who introduced herself to me as Amanda Woods, whose real name is Ellie Franklin. I called Sam to see if he would call Joey's mother and send Joey Ellie

Franklin's picture to see if it was the same woman. He said
he would. I waited a few minutes, and then I called her.
She put Joey on the phone. Joey said he thinks it is the
same woman, but it was dark when she came, and he can't
be sure. He said someone was with her, but he has no idea
if it was a man or a woman. Of course, Joey has no idea if
the woman went to the Oxley house or not. But if it is the
same woman, it would be too much of a coincidence to say
she went somewhere else instead.

I called Sam back and told him what Joey said. He gave me
Ellie Franklin's phone number. I called her to see what
story she would give me this time.

"Is this Ellie Franklin, alias Amanda Woods?"

"You must be the man who questioned me at the
resort. What do you want this time?"

"Why did you lie to me?"

"I like that movie. I like Cameron Diaz. And I was
trying to find out what happened to my sister. I'm still
trying to find out."

"And you're still claiming she was your sister?"

"She was. In a way. My dad lived with her mom for a
few years, so we started calling each other sister. We were
closer than a lot of sisters."

"Were you ever in Hilldale, Kentucky?"

"Why do you ask that?"

"Because someone identified you as being there, at
the house where your sister's body was found."

"My sister was murdered there?"

"You act as though you don't know that."

"I didn't. I knew she loved the books that couple
writes. I think someone took her and Drake there. I don't
know that for sure, but I think they did. Amanda said
something about going to visit the Oxleys with another fan
of theirs. She didn't tell me who. And then I didn't hear
from her again. I followed her there, in a manner of
speaking. I even went up to the house and knocked, but no
one came to the door. So, I left."

"Did you go alone?"

"I stayed with a friend of mine who lives in Kentucky. She didn't think what I was doing was safe. She drove me there. She waited in the car. It was dark, so when no one answered the door, I waited a couple of minutes, and then I left. Amanda said something about coming up to the place where I met you, where some other home swappers would be. She told me the dates they would be there, so I waited around and eventually went up there."

"Someone said they saw you in North Carolina first."

"You have good sources. Yes. I was in Tennessee and North Carolina before I went up there. My friend didn't go with me."

"And now you are back to selling real estate."

"They are having a memorial service for Amanda and Drake in a few days. I will be going to that. I haven't made up my mind yet if I will tell them who I am."

"Won't your dad and her mom be there?"

"My dad died of cancer. Her mom drowned in a boating accident a couple of years ago. I don't think there will be anyone there who knows me."

"What name will you use when you go?"

"I'm not sure yet. I have three IDs. I'll make it up as I go."

I told her goodbye and ended the call. I wondered if she was still making up what she told me and if she murdered the four people whose murders I was trying to solve. If it comes to it, I'm sure I can track her down.

+++

I told the others I didn't want to be bothered while I thought about the case. I went into the other room and put the five photographs on the bed. I picked them up one at a time and looked at them. The more I stared at them, the more I was sure I had met all five, some time or other when I was walking around the property. I just didn't recognize three of them. I looked at those three. Was one of them someone I saw while Lou and I were showing off our expertise with a tomahawk or a bow and arrow? Could one of them be the woman I met who was a little rude when I went into a shop? Was one of them the guy who said he was there for the card convention? With each passing hour, memories of the people I met were fading away. But I was sure I met most or all of them.

I continued to stare at the pictures, and then I read what was beneath each picture or what Sam told me when I talked to him. And I tried to think of what Karl and Kristin Olson said when I talked to them. And then it hit me. I thought I knew who the killer was. I looked at one of the pictures again. That could be the murderer. I needed to make a phone call, and if that call turned out the way I expected, I needed to make a second call.

A few minutes later, after three phone calls to verify what I wanted to know at the first place I planned to call instead of just one call, I knew enough to make the second phone call. I made it and talked to a couple of people. I asked them not to say anything about what I called about.

I went into the other room and gathered the troops. I told them I was almost certain as to who the murderer is. Or is it three murderers? At any rate, we were going to check this out in next morning, contact the state authorities, and head out to arrest a murderer or see that one is arrested. After that, we would be heading home to pray that no one else is murdered in Hilldale, or with any connection to Hilldale.

32

We ate breakfast the next morning, loaded the van, checked out, and left Mohonk Mountain House behind. Lou and I cried as we realized that it might be a while before we threw another tomahawk or paddleboarded. Jennifer and Thelma Lou tried to console us. Both promised to buy us kayaks for Christmas. I told Jennifer I would give mine to Quiggley as soon as the Foundation okayed us to have a pool.

We drove past some beautiful scenery that we had never seen. I had to keep my eyes on the road. Otherwise, I might get to look at the scenery much closer than I wanted. I hoped that each person who had a copy of *Bad Swap* was able to read it and that each person who left the resort we had shared was still breathing.

+++

When we got to our destination, I located the state police. I explained the situation and showed them my credentials. I told them that I needed them to find a place for the murderer until they could be transported to Kentucky for trial. Two officers referred me to the local authorities who directed us to the place we sought.

I went to the door and knocked. The door was answered by someone I didn't recognize, but I knew who it was. I had seen that person in three other disguises a few days previously. She jumped slightly when she saw me, before composing herself.

"Hello, Maggie. Sorry, but that's the first name I knew you as. You look a lot younger now. You looked much younger the two other times you bumped into me in the resort and called me Cy. But now I know you are Barb Linkenfelter, owner of this bed-and-breakfast. You shouldn't have been so violent when you told Karl and Kristen Olson how much you hated home swaps, or you should have murdered them before they told me about you. Otherwise, you might not have gotten caught."

"I don't know what you're talking about."

"Sure you do. You killed them at Mohonk Mountain House."

"I've never been there."

"Oh, but you have. You were photographed leaving there, just after you killed them. They have a nice picture of your license plate, and one of you wearing the disguise you wore at the time. And you made the mistake of leaving fingerprints in their room."

"I don't think so."

"Oh, but you did. Not on the syringe. But on the book. You touched the book before you went into their room. You didn't put on the gloves until they opened their door to you. And you did the same in Kentucky."

"I didn't leave a book in Kentucky."

"Oops! I think you just gave something away. And now, these two men are going to take you away and keep you until we can extradite you to Kentucky for the first of your murders. Or was it the first?"

"Those home swappers are ruining my business. They said they weren't coming back again. I have to have enough money to live on."

"We have a system that will take care of you from now on. That will not be a problem. We won't know until after your trial just how long that will be."

"Let me get my things, and I will be with you."

"I don't think so. Either you will try to sneak out the back, or you will bring a syringe or some other kind of weapon back with you. It's not cold. You don't need a wrap."

"But I have guests."

"We will take care of the guests. They might have to check out sooner than they expected, but we will let them know how lucky they are."

"I have never harmed any of my guests."

"Maybe not while they were staying with you. I'll admit you were patient. It was a while since either couple stayed here."

"I was hoping they would change their mind and come back."

"Well, we're not changing our minds. Barb Linkfelter, you are under arrest for the murders of four people."

She put up a fight, but we subdued her. She was put in the back of the Vermont police car and whisked away. I went in and found her guests, who hadn't heard our confrontation at the front door. I told them that Miss Linkenfelter had been called away unexpectedly and would not be returning soon, and they would have to leave in the morning.

On the way to her house, I explained to the others about my two phone calls. I found out that Drake and Amanda Peabody had stayed a couple of times at her bed-and-breakfast before discovering home swapping. I found out by calling the Actors Guild in Vermont that Barb Linkenfelter had played some small parts in a few plays and was quite adept at makeup and making characters look completely different than the way they normally look. I was sure that she was the old woman who introduced herself to me as Maggie, and probably both of the other women who knew my name whom I had never seen before. I wasn't sure what disguise she wore when she murdered those two people. She probably posed as a maid and the face was not her own.

+++

There was no way we were staying at the bed-and-breakfast. She might have a demented son we knew nothing about. We found an inn nearby and headed home the next morning. We took our time going home. There was too much of a chance that the Chief might call me about another murder.

33

We had already checked out of Mohonk Mountain House, so we weren't going back there. Although I would consider it a delightful place to stay if you have a lot of money and you don't have to solve a murder while you are there.

We took a vote, and it was unanimous. It was time to go home and rest. But at our age, we weren't going to set a world record for getting home in the least amount of time. We would take two or three days to get home.

+++

We got home a few days later and found Quiggley frolicking in the hot tub. She was having the time of her life. But I could tell she missed us. As soon as we rounded the corner of the house, she flew out of there and flapped her wings heading in our direction. She landed at our feet. Jennifer stroked her feathers for a minute or two then headed off to make sure she hadn't run out of food or water. We had stopped on the way home at a place where Jennifer picked up some dog and duck treats. Jennifer made over the duck while I headed inside to make sure there were no ruffled feathers inside. And no duck eggs. I had already checked to make sure that Quiggley hadn't invited someone over for a sleepover. At least if she did, he left before we returned.

+++

I was awakened the next morning by someone opening the bedroom door. A woman who looked familiar entered, carrying a lap tray full of breakfast food. I noticed that she was wearing something that wasn't suitable for church. That was fine. It wasn't Sunday.

"To what do I owe this pleasure?"

"Are you talking about me or the food?"

"Oh, is there food too?"

"If I wasn't afraid of you spilling it, I would cuff you up the side of the head."

She moved around to the other side of the bed and slipped under the covers beside me before answering my question.

"You seemed to enjoy breakfast in bed so much at that fancy place in New York that I thought I would treat you to the same at home. And we don't have to rush off to solve a murder."

"I'll eat fast."

"Don't hurry. We have a few things to discuss."

"Like what?"

"Well, while you were sleeping I signed us up for a pickleball league."

"A what?"

"I'll give you the details later."

"It sounds like there is exercise involved."

"A little, but you'll like it. And you'll know one of the other couples."

"Do they live nearby?"

"Quite nearby."

"Does he know yet?"

"He's receiving his breakfast and his news now too."

"Did you sign us up for anything else?"

"No, but there is a dog to pick up."

"That mangy mutt. I can get him later."

"It's all taken care of. Thelma Lou and I will get him later."

"How about this afternoon?"

"Aren't you going to eat? And if the phone rings, there won't be any reason to answer it. It won't be Lou or Thelma Lou."

"She'll be explaining to him what pickleball is?"

"Something like that."

+++

I refrained from going over and asking my neighbor how his breakfast was while the girls went and collected a spoiled dog. Blue came home and frolicked with Quiggley in the backyard. Jennifer and I enjoyed the animals for a while, then went inside. Blue would come in when he was ready. Jennifer and I picked up a couple of books we hadn't gotten to and began to read. After an hour or so, we both came up for air, talked, and said that we had made a good choice. Jennifer, never as tired as I am, said she would rather cook than go out for dinner. We ate, read for a while longer, and went to bed a little earlier than usual. Traveling does that to me.

The morning after that, Jennifer and I slept in. Blue did too. In his bed in the living room. I would wait a couple of more days before calling the Chief to let him know that the murders were solved, and we were back at home. That was just in case there had been another murder and he was looking for someone to solve it. If there had been one, I was going to tell him to put an ad in the paper. I told Jennifer that, and she told me that isn't the way it's done anymore. Some things don't change enough, while other things change too much. I appear to be on the wrong end of both of them.

+++

The next day, our bodies were getting back to normal. I knew that because Jennifer suggested a walk in the woods. I suggested waiting one more day. Instead, I said something about spending some time on the front porch swing after breakfast, recommended taking her to the Blue Moon for lunch, and then coming home for a nap, a movie, and picking up a mystery to read and solve that didn't require me to move out of my chair to do that. Jennifer was agreeable to all of that. She asked me if any of that involved the neighbors. I told her only the trip to the Blue Moon. She asked me if she was allowed to interrupt me if I was reading. I said it depended on what she had in mind. She said it wouldn't involve me helping her wash dishes. I told her I would consider other possibilities.

+++

After a few more days at home, we decided to drive to Lexington and spend part of the day there. We came in on Winchester Road and Man O War, and when we passed Hamburg and all it has to offer, Jennifer suggested we stop at Costco before heading home. That was fine with the rest of us. We each had our cell phones in case we got separated. Lou and I wandered up one aisle and down another until we found something that interested us. Snacks. We had a buggy in case we found something we wanted. Lou immediately saw a big plastic jar of M&Ms. I was surprised when he only got two jars.

"Well, we might not be coming back for a couple of weeks."

Almost next to it was a jar of the same size filled with chocolate-covered almonds. I showed more restraint. I put only one jar in the buggy. We looked around to see if we could find anything else that could use a temporary home, but our wives' radar was up and they came up our aisle with a buggy half full of the biggest chicken pot pie ever seen outside of a town festival, and another that looked similar, which Jennifer said was shepherd's pie. I'd had that before and liked it. I saw they also had a jar of M&Ms for Lou and one of chocolate-covered almonds for me. They had a few other snacks too, plus a couple of other things for dinner. I was hoping the dinner items were heading to my house. We shopped for a few more minutes, and then it was time to head home and rest until someone else was murdered. I hope it is twenty years before that happens. I was sure the Chief could find someone half as good as me by then. As we were loading what we bought into my van, Lou had Thelma Lou open his M&Ms and take the cardboard off so he could eat some on the way home.

"Can't you take it off, yourself?"

"My fingernails aren't long enough."

"It's not hard. Here, Jennifer," I said as I handed her my chocolate-covered almonds. "Show him how easy it is to get the cardboard off."

Author's Note

While I hadn't done this before, I planted some clues in this book to let you know who the murderer is. Some of them were before Cy went to the first murder scene.

1) To let you know that the murderer changed disguises, I mentioned that Cy and Jennifer watched Tootsie, Mrs. Doubtfire, and Kind Hearts and Coronets. Each of them has an actor who plays more than one character.
2) One of the people that Cy met on the way to New York was a guy who was an actor who specialized in makeup and making people look different.
3) Another person Cy met was playing a Rod Stewart song in his car. One of Stewart's songs is Maggie May.
4) Karl and Kristin Olson mention having a problem with a woman who runs a bed-and-breakfast. She didn't like that they were doing home swapping instead.

If you weren't able to pick up on the clues and identify the murderer well before the end, don't kick yourself. None of my proofreaders picked up on the clues either.

Made in United States
Cleveland, OH
04 January 2025

13063548R00132